Cease To Exist

TABLE OF CONTENTS

Cease To Exist

~ Book Overview ~

A woman is trapped in her life and discovers that she must fight to stay alive while gaining the strength to tell her story of self-defense in the murder of her wealthy husband and the death of her only child. Naomi Kilpatrick is a beautiful young woman who must ultimately reside as a stranger in the sleepy unassuming town that she grew up in. She has chosen this place to dwell as a way to re-connect with her catastrophic past and start anew. If this issue is not laid to rest, she is certain it will greedily engulf her along with all of her ambitions and dreams she possess for the future. The thought of moving forward for her at this time of her life is like trying to climb Mount Everest with a broken leg and no climbing gear.

It is humanly impossible. With the fate that awaits her in tow, Naomi's life takes a turn for the worse and her shocking past becomes her present, which, if not altered threatens to destroy her future. She must hold on for dear life in order to survive. Before she can advance forward, she must plummet backwards in time journeying through her childhood and young adulthood picking up fragmented pieces of her life to guide her through this miserable state of existence. Naomi knows she must unravel her past quickly in order to stay among the living. Her quest is to return to the only safe haven she knows which will be the one place that will bring her back to the reality she needs in order to fast forward past her futile situation and once again reside where the coast is clear in the land of the living. "She dreams herself back to life"

Author: Victoria E. Kain

Cease To Exist

Author: | *Victoria E. Kain*
Photography | Graphic Illustrations by: |*www.gritography.com*
Layout Design by: | *Andrew Simon*
Global Marketing Division: | *Jane Adams*
Publisher: | *Fycore Publishing*

www.fycore.com

International Publisher Author Number:	1403427755160
International Standard Book Number	SB:	9781619100053
International Standard Book Number	HB:	9781619100244
International Digital eBook Number:	9781619100237
Library of Congress Control Number:	2014931289

Additional Formats May be Available for Pre-Order:

PHYSICAL		DIGITAL	
Trade Cloth	$39.95	CD/MP3 (Audio Book)	$19.95
Hard Back	$29.95	PDF Book	$16.95
Soft Back	$18.95	eBook	$9.99

For Inquiries or Additional Orders:

131 Sunset Ave Ste E#353
Suisun City CA, 94585
Office | (800) 470-FYCORE
Facsimile: | (800) 531-0190
Email: | publisher@fycore.com

www.fycore.com

Fycore Publishing

4th Book Edition from the
"I'll be Brief" Series

I'LL **B**E RIEF

TM

"Great Minds Read Between the Lines"

Author: Victoria E. Kain

Cease To Exist

Author's Perspective
by: Victoria E. Kain

A spider's web is weaved with instinctive precision. The preparation and timing of each strand being spun is calculated to minutia. We can only perceive what the end result of this systemic effort will produce for the eight legged creature that inhabits it. By rationalizing the sophistication of how it will protect, transport, provide sustenance, and a delicate form of communication for its inhabitant, you only have to observe the spider itself. Without the specific components of this design for a spider's web, they would simply become a "defenseless insect waiting to become something else's prey."

Synonymous to this analogy is; human life. It is likened to the Spider's web because it requires many of the very same major components. Without love, security, comfort, communication or nourishment, life cannot exist. Having no hiding place from the storms of life, Naomi Kilpatrick is ultimately left without the human core needs from her biological mother and ultimately her husband to sustain her physical and mental existence. These two people robbed her of the emotional stability that would help sustain and protect her when all she had in this world was being ripped from her beating heart. She became the vulnerable prey to the ultimate unsuspecting predator, "life." How will she survive the madness of living? Only one thing can bring her back.

Dedication

This book is dedicated to my brother Michael, family and friends. "I love you and I am very proud of you" are words seldom spoken in the human family. If life sometimes makes you feel as if you have "ceased to exist," then it's time to reinvent yourself to regain the courage to survive "living." A simple kind word or deed goes a long way to healing the wounded souls of those who have been made to feel "invisible." The journey in life is different for all of us, but it does matter how we chose to travel the roads we are destined to encounter.

*We must remember that "**Love**" is the captive spirit in our lives. Embrace "it" and the good times and with personalized hip boots we will wade through the bad. Accepting any and all love given to us by those that choose to show us kindness even though they may be considered strangers to us. Doing so will always help us until we finally plant both feet back on solid ground for a firmer stance to a brighter future. Remember to tell your story over and over again until it is believed and embraced by everyone that hears it...and last of all...always give yourself permission to "Dream Out Loud."*

"I love you all"

Author: Victoria E. Kain

~ A Memory of Better Days ~

As she swiftly walked through the pages of her mind, thinking that she had all the answers, she was sadly mistaken when she found that she hadn't a clue as to what really existed in her heart. One minute she imagined seeing something clearly, the next minute brought her into a stark reality that she was mentally blind and saw nothing at all. Have you ever desperately searched for something you couldn't find, only to give up searching and immediately find it? You play the scenario over and over in your head, rewinding the events again and again, of how you searched effortlessly only to glance over in an unsuspecting area, and there the item sits…mysteriously staring you right in the face.

We sometimes stop for a moment in amazement trying to figure out how we missed what should have been blatantly obvious. Our lives are the same way. We miss the obvious and struggle to find things that were never lost…When this happens, we have simply failed to recognize that what we thought was lost was not valued enough to keep it in our present memory. The human brain is amazing. It quickly discards things that appear to have no further use to us. Thereby clearing our memory for things in our lives that truly will make a difference for us. Have you ever felt that way? Naomi's brain did the same to her and the people in her life… There were twists and turns that took her into new realms of existence every second from the time she was five years old until her biological clock began ticking out of control.

Cease To Exist

What is a spider without its web? Someone had asked this question of her years earlier before her situation deteriorated to the point of her finding the true answer. She simply could not fathom a response, but years later, the understanding was clear. Without a web, the spider is a defenseless insect waiting to become something else's prey. Humans are preyed upon every day by the societies we live in. We must find our own mechanisms for survival.

At times we must become like the "Chameleon," calculating our every move knowing we only have seconds to adapt to our new environment or we will cease to exist, never to be remembered again. What lengths will we go to in order to make it to the next hour, minute, or second of the day. How desperate do we become when tragedy strikes and introduces itself as our new uninvited bedfellow. Ultimately, time takes its ugly toll on all our lives and causes us to recoil from the misery of fate as it engulfs us like it did Jonah in the belly of the big fish.... Yet, even he, later emerged anew, full of hopes and dreams of survival. Naomi can only wish that she will gain her life back in one piece and save her future.

Author: Victoria E. Kain

~ CHAPTER 1 ~

The Long Journey Home

Naomi was awakened by the sound of police sirens outside her bedroom window. In a weakened state, curiosity had gotten the best of her as she struggled to raise herself up to the window near her bed to see where the flashing police lights were coming from. She leaned towards the window sill and pulled back the thick curtains that covered the two large panes. Before she is clear of anything, her mind reeled back to better days of looking out of the same window. As she pulled back the curtains, she slowly moved the blanket that covered her frail body to place her feet on the thick shag rug that lay next to the bed. As the covers were lightly tossed aside with what little strength she had, what her eyes beheld next was unmentionable in her mind. Naomi gasped as she caught sight of the dark red blood stains that covered her satin sheets...

Instant fear struck all over her body and gave a surge of energy as she feverishly threw back the covers completely with all her might. She wanted to know what this horrible sight was that she was embracing in the cortex of her brain. "Are they coming for me? She frantically sought the exit wounds where the blood could have been coming from on her sheets. Now becoming faint, she continued to search her body, groping in places on herself as if she were two people desperately trying to find any open wound, wanting to know what had produced the large amount of blood that had soaked into the light colored carpet on the floor.

It had now made the bed where she laid wet and sticky to the touch. Finally she accepted there were no exit wounds on her body that could be visibly seen. Even with the evidence there, she simply could not accept that analogy completely. Still in a weakened state, she knew there had to be something done to produce this blood she could see and smell. Fear had turned into panic and she was becoming weaker as the room began to spin from what she witnessed. The next physiological process was right on time. She began trembling uncontrollably. Her stomach churned the contents of her insides as her limbs grew numb from her waist down and finally… she could not move at all. As she struggled to stay cognizant, she wearily turned her attention to the sound of sirens outside that were getting closer to her home as she began to fade into darkness. At this point, there was no way to stop the process. She was going into shock. Before she completely lost all consciousness, she mentally accepted the fact that the sirens heard in a distance were now in her front yard.

She could hear her heart beating in her chest so loudly and with such force that it drowned out the batter ram at the front door. The clock kept ticking in her head. She rolled over to the edge of the bed to raise herself erect as the door was caved in by six men in police uniforms. What happened next was horrifying. She would not know why they had come for her as she faded into darkness once again. But this time, the darkness she would inhabit would linger for a long time and ultimately shed light on her life in a horrifying way.

Author: Victoria E. Kain

Cease To Exist

Time is an amazing thing. You cannot store it, you cannot harness it and when it is gone, you can never get it back. When you think you have all of the answers to questions in your life, you quickly find that you haven't got a clue as to what really exists. Think about it for a moment... Have you ever thought you saw something clearly only to realize that what you saw was strangely different than what you imagined when you finally see it? The stark reality is that we are legally blind and see nothing at all when our emotions and fear take over. Our emotions can be an anchor for us in a time of need if we can control them, but most of us simply succumb to our fears which cause our senses to be dulled instantly.

Whenever this happens, our brain scrambles all our signals and distorts the messages we receive causing us to desperately search to make sense out of things we experience in life. Even then, we fail miserably to get things right the first time. Why do we search for things we want to find, but as soon as we give up searching, we find it? When we stop exerting so much effort looking for what we want, the sad reality is that it will usually find us still sitting in the same lonely place we always sat in, wishing for the best while we wait for our proverbial ship to come in. Only to soon realize after years of waiting and watching, that our ship had docked many moons ago...completely unnoticed by us.

Cease To Exist

Naomi Kilpatrick is one of those who waited in the darkness of her mind and longed for her uncertain future that awaited her. Life for her would mimic the Spider's existence. She would instinctively know when to find the right time to weave her web to create a safe haven. Acquiring the necessary comforts and protection from the predators that would easily take advantage of her in this weakened state, she would weave a fine web. She knew that like the spider, without this web she would become helpless and defenseless and would soon become someone else's prey.

When Naomi was not able to protect herself from the tragedies in her life she became defenseless. She was struck with many traumas and could simply no longer comprehend the task of staying among the living, yet she did everything to stay alive. Her mind was forced to shut down as a way to preserve her heart. She knew what her body could not handle. What does it mean to be a defenseless human? Naomi would find a shocking way to survive. Two will tell her story, but only one will live it.

Author: Victoria E. Kain

~ CHAPTER 2 ~

Where It All Began

Canoga Springs, Nevada is a small country town with all the old charm of years gone by. It is located in an area that seems to be in the middle of nowhere but is surrounded by everything imaginable. It is in the middle of summer and even with the futility of the location to its distance from other civilization, it is thought by scores of people to be one of the most beautiful places you will ever want to see in your life time. People flock to our little town from many miles away to vacation with their families or just couples renewing their marriage vows.

They want to feel the old world charm of this almost extinct existence of a place likened to paradise. People arrive here, they become free of all the unnecessary. When they carry around with them in the cities where they came from. There is no hustle and bustle of rapid transit trains, accidents, busses, six lane freeways that clog the city during rush hour. In this town, they get the subtle feeling that everyone knows each other by the way people greet one another on the street as if they are all old friends. They want to feel that same warmth as if they are also old friends of these people who reside here. They smile and greet each other as if they truly treasured seeing the stranger and would look forward to seeing them again. This type of positive attitude is what makes life good for most of us here as residents in this little town and makes visitors wish this had been the place they were born.

Cease To Exist

The old shops are nestled between the beautiful old tree lined streets and strangely enough, many elderly people walk about as if they are in the prime of life. It is rare to see walkers or canes or the aged hobbling about slowly, not knowing what direction to go in. There are only mature healthy people with silver streaked hair and preppy clothing for their age group that denoted a well secured and happy life having been and still being lived to the full.

They are all well cared for people out for a morning stroll, getting a cup of java at the corner café. They pass by Mr. Campbell, who owns the bakery which connects to the only coffee shop in town. Across from that is the butcher shop owned by Mr. Pete. Now, Mr. Pete is a strange man with an interesting story that he tells everyone he meets. He is kind in every way but very quiet until you start him chattering. The story he tells is that he came to America as a migrant worker and had learned carpentry from his adoptive parents.   Although he never learned to read or write, he could measure and count in his head the feet and inches of a board to the exact measure of what was needed to build any structure. No one ever knew who his parents were or whether he had brothers or sisters. He met his future wife one day while wandering through the countryside looking for work and stumbled across this family. He was hired by the owner who had a beautiful young daughter, and on that first day he affectionately called her "Sugar."

Author: Victoria E. Kain

After working a while for the farmer, he told him that he was going to marry his little girl. His account almost sounds like the biblical story where a man had to work to earn the money to marry the farmer's youngest daughter. He fell in love with her but because she had an older sister, he ended up with two wives. This was not a case of bigamy, but was of divine arrangement that the older daughter had to be married first, ultimately giving the man two wives. Well, Mr. Pete only ended up with the one wife he wanted, and that was "Sugar."

He knew that sugar was the one the first time he laid eyes on her at her father's farm. Being of Asian descent, he was a man of his word. He first worked, saved his money and bought and paid for four acres of land on a beautiful road. He married Sugar and they lived with another farm owner until their home was built. Mr. Pete continued to work and build his own home for him and Sugar. He was such a good carpenter that many contractors wanted to hire him. He was given free lumber from the carpentry jobs he had where the owners may have miss-cut wood and could not use it. Because he did not drive, his ride would drop him off along with the lumber he'd been given for the day and he would stay there and build on his house until almost night fall and then he would walk home to Sugar. He pulled old nails out of abandoned houses and reused them in his building project and bought others.

Cease To Exist

Finally Pete and Sugar had a beautiful country home. It had screened doors and windows, two bedrooms, a living room and a big country kitchen with a wood burning stove with a warming oven. This was truly a luxury if you lived in the country where most people had open doors and windows with flies and gnats coming in and out at will. This would not be the case for Sugar. She would always have the best that Pete could afford. Mr. Pete even put in a big swing on the front porch for Sugar.

She would sit out there every evening after dinner and Mr. Pete would lie on the other end of the porch and nap comfortably. For cold winters, Mr. Pete built two fireplaces with one chimney. This was an amazing old house and a beautiful story. As the years passed, they had one son and the three of them lived happily in that old house. Eventually their son grew up and took a wife of his own and moved away to the city. Sugar wanted to be in town for better shopping and to be closer to her son so Mr. Pete moved into town and took the money he had saved for many years and bought the butcher shop down in Canoga Springs. He could never say no to Sugar and the two of them have lived here ever since. Sugar now cooks hot biscuits and tea cakes each morning at the butcher shop and they are the best you can eat. Everyone knows that the town workers can get a free hot biscuit and ham from five to seven a.m.

Author: Victoria E. Kain

Cease To Exist

This was Mr. Pete's idea because he remembered how it was when he came to America to work and many days he did not have money for food. Now, if you wanted fresh honey to go with those biscuits from Pete and Sugar, Joey McFarland and his wife Patty owned the bee hives in the town. People came from miles around to get the honey. The McFarland's refused to sell it on the grocery market. They always said that it tasted better when it was local grown and local eaten. No one knew what that really meant, but they knew it was the best in the town. They also knew that McFarland's mother, Candice McFarland was there every evening.

She sat outside the old store like a gentle guard dog that would let nothing trouble its owners. Everyone knew she would not hurt a fly, but they weren't so sure about that old walking cane that never left her side in her 85 years of living. Either way, if she didn't have to hurt you for any reason, you could get a slice of her homemade lemon pound cake. It made her day for people to rant and rave about her pound cake from a recipe her mother gave her when she was only 14 years old. Needless to say, the recipe was as authentic as her cane. Folks always thought she sat outside the store because she was lonely and wanted company, so everyone stopped and talked to her. There were three rocking chairs in front of the store and every year they painted them a different color.

Cease To Exist

The chairs looked as if they have had fifty coats of paint on them but it made them look cleaner and added cushion I suppose. Mother McFarland occupied one of the chairs and that left two for town folk or tourists to sit and relax from their sightseeing in the town. Occasionally they took pictures. She really loved that. The town did not seem to have many children but today there seemed to be a few of us kids riding bikes since school was out. They all were very polite to say excuse me if they were walking or had to stop abruptly. The politeness exhibited was like something you would see in a Norman Rockwell painting. I had lived here all of my life and was always soothed by the shear relaxed atmosphere of this town. I had hoped that one day I could raise my children here if I was fortunate enough to find the right man.

It was too early to tell what would happen to me since I was still young. I knew I wanted to live here forever. The scenery was breathtaking and it was where people came to break the monotony of their hectic lives in the city. For me, it was simply home. I never dreamed that things could be prettier anywhere else. I guess I never thought much of myself either. But, Nana always said I was her beautiful little girl. She said I had the prettiest blue eyes she had ever seen, although they were exactly like my Mamas eyes. I think she just told me that to make me feel good. It always seemed to work. My ponytails were very long this year. They reached down to my waist.

Author: Victoria E. Kain

I had curly bangs that caused my face to be like a full moon. My cheeks were rosy and when I smiled Nana said I could light up a room. I was still a bit shy as well for a girl my age. Most girls were already dating. I always loved to hear Nana talk to me about how pretty she thought I was since I never heard nice things like that from Mama. I guess she really didn't love me, but I knew Nana did. Even though I wanted to live in this town forever, I also wanted to travel to a big city and see all sorts of different things like a city sky line, bright lights, fast cars and even traffic jams. We never saw that in our little town. I wanted to experience the wealth of what people considered as "having it all."

But for now, I would be happy living with my parents and visiting Nana and Grandpa every summer. Today though, since they came to see us and are in town to shop, Mama reluctantly let me go with them. She was going to get her hair done today. She always thought that Nana would spoil me with things that she never had when she was a little girl and that upset her. I loved doing anything with Nana because I knew she truly loved me. Being the youngest of three siblings and the only one left at home caused some heart aches that were unique to me not being the "only" child, but I was glad my step brothers had moved away to college and gone into the Military. There was not much interaction with them since they were much older.

Everyone always talked around me as if I couldn't hear at all. I would over hear them say, "Naomi was Peggy's late life baby." At the time that I heard this, I didn't realize it but they were saying that my mother was in the "change" of life. She was going into menopause. Naomi wondered why they called it men-o-pause and rationalized that it was a time that women stopped having anything to do with men. She still did not understand, but thought it anyway. She quickly realized that this could not be the case because mama had friends who were men and then, there was daddy. This showed Naomi's naivety. She also discerned that her father was much younger than her mother which would account for much of the arguing they did.

She also was her father's only biological child that Mama had. You would think that this would have made her mama happy that she had given him a child, but Naomi always felt her mother did not want her around and always sent her to Nana's every summer to get rid of her. She didn't mind because she loved Nana and Grandpa Cody and welcomed the break from being home with mama. The fact that this weekend Nana and Grandpa Cody had come to town to shop and were going to take me back home with them was a treat. This would be the beginning of my summer vacation and a memorable time as well. It wasn't often that I got to shop with Nana in town since this was the reason I was in town at all. I normally am not permitted to go anywhere without Mama, unless it is with Nana.

It was as if Mama trusted no one with me but Nana. But today, Nana won the argument as to why I should go with her and Grandpa Cody. Mama always got her hair done on Saturday's and it didn't make sense to Nana for me to sit in the hair salon when I was not getting my hair done. I really didn't care because I was going to Nana's when we finished shopping in town today and my summer vacation would begin with a bang. I sat in the back of the old station wagon that was outdated... I really didn't care what year the vehicle was. I was happy just going somewhere away from the house.

The fact still remained that I never went further than home and to my Nana's house every summer after the boys left home. My brother Jared was the knee baby as they called him since he was the one next to me. He went into the Army and he rarely came home. Someone said he had gone to jail in the stockade but no one talked about it around me. They just pretended it didn't happen...I knew there had to be a reason why he never came home and he was always what they called a "Mama's boy," who couldn't be away from Mama for too long without coming back. That was a dead giveaway for me.

Cease To Exist

Being out of school on summer vacation was all I lived for because it gave me the rare opportunity not to be cooped up at home where I was always alone and frustrated. Not having siblings made me very lonely at times but I had my thoughts, my dolls, Nana and my dreams which seemed to get more intense every year. All the other kids had scores of brothers and sisters and cousins, but I had no one. Despite the fact that I lived in a fancy middle class neighborhood with all the trimmings, my grandmother's house was the place where I dreamed of living forever. "Humph!" Naomi said. Most folk would rate Nana's house next to nothing more than a shack, I'll bet! But to me, this house had more love, character and charm than any of the new houses I had ever lived in since I was born.

I always felt that someday this house would be a place of happiness for me and would save my life. I wondered what the kids in the neighborhood were doing on this beautiful Saturday since no one came to pick them up and take them to town or anywhere, she thought. "If they could see me now, I know they'd be jealous." They all just stayed at home every summer and did work around the house. Sort of like what I did during the school year to pass the time when mama was at work. Some of the kids might be able to go to the movies at least once or twice but that would be it. Most of them in her neighborhood were from single parent homes and I was the only kid on the block that had both parents for what that was worth.

Author: Victoria E. Kain

Everything Naomi heard about her Mama and her daddy, she wondered about it. Someone had said that they married only because she was pregnant with me. Mama was concerned about how people would view an older woman with a baby by a younger man if they were just living together. It was a sad thing to think this is what I heard. The neighbor kids thought Naomi was special and believed she should be flawlessly happy because she had both parents and didn't have brothers and sisters to share with. They just didn't know how Naomi really felt on the inside. During the school year, Naomi would busy herself after school and played with her dolls and kept to herself. The large bedroom that she slept in made her afraid of the dark at night, because she thought it felt like a tomb.

She stared at the pink and blue curtains every day she would wake up. She hated the color blue for some strange reason and to top it off, her bed covers were blue as well with tiny stars with red stripes. She often wondered why her room had to resemble the star spangle banner but quickly realized that her dad was in the military so Mama probably wanted him to think that I really cared about him being a soldier. I really didn't care about the military because daddy was always gone and I couldn't understand that at all. I wanted him home. Either way, I had to abide by their rule which was to be patriotic even though I didn't understand war and why my dad had to go overseas all the time. I always thought that was why my older brother joined.

It seemed as if mama wanted the perfect family and this was to be the perfect life. "But for who?" I thought, patiently sitting in the back of the car while Grandpa Cody finally found a parking space in front of the old mill store for Nana to go in and get her supplies. I was tired of daydreaming about my boring life and realized that he must have circled a hundred times to wait until someone came out of the store to get right at the front door. Nana had hip problems and didn't like to walk far so she rattled Grandpas' cage until he finally got the spot at the door. I wouldn't be going in with Nana in this store since she was picking up her supplies and there was nothing in there for me to do. "You stay in the car with Grandpa, Naomi." She said.

"Yes ma'am," I stated, looking out the window at the other folk going into the store and coming out with bags of feed for their cattle and other goods.

I wanted Nana to hurry up and come out of the feed store so we could go to the clothing store she always goes to that had things for the whole family. It was not like food wasn't for the whole family, but this was a clothing store where kids' things were sold, in my size! Nana was out in a flash and Grandpa got out and put the packages in the back of the station wagon. He hurried back in the driver's seat where he always was because Nana didn't drive. "Where to now, woman?" he asked her.

"You know I want to go to the clothing factory Cody," Nana said, semi rolling her eyes, but being careful not to let Grandpa see her do it. She knew he would get upset and not want to bring her to town the next time if she did that. He was funny about things like that.

"I wanted to be sure Mattie," he said, pushing his cap back off his face. Grandpa always did that when he was getting restless or upset. He had bad knees and a bad back and couldn't sit for long but he made sure he took Nana where she wanted to go. She always said he was jealous of her, but I thought they were just in love with each other. Besides she didn't ask for much.

We finally came up to the store and a parking space opened up right in front of the door again. "Hot dog!" Nana said. That was her spunky talk when she felt as if she had gotten exactly what she wanted. We all were happy when Nana was happy. She looked back and asked.

"You want to come in with me baby?" She said. I was grinning like a Cheshire cat; I quickly accepted her offer to ensure she didn't change her mind.

"Yes ma'am," I said, jumping out of the car before she could change her mind. "Gal, watch where you going!" she scolded.

"There are cars coming in this parking lot!"

"I sure don't want to explain to your Mama if you get hit by one of them."

Slowing my walk down to almost a crawl, I politely responded to her.

Cease To Exist

"Yes, ma'am," I said, grabbing Nana by the hand as if to reassure her that she was in full control and I was there right by her side. I didn't want anything to stop me from going into this store. As we walked towards the door, I could feel a warm breeze move softly across my face. It felt good to be out and about on Saturday. Mama really didn't take me anywhere and I hoped it wouldn't scar me for life by not getting out more. She always shopped for me and brought me what she wanted me to have. I felt I was old enough to have some privileges but she gave me none.

Nana was different. It seemed that she was proud to take me everywhere she went. I was like her pride and joy. Once we were in the store, I looked around to see what was new…everything was new to me because I had not been there in a while. My eyes absorbed everything. Grabbing like a greedy hand all the pretty colors of the clothing and toys, looking at the new items that the store had for children and I even looked at something for Mama, even though I didn't have any money to spend today, I still thought about her.

"What would I get today?" I thought. Nana always bought me something. We began shopping for material for Nana to sew. 'Is she going to make me a dress?' I thought or maybe she is making aprons for the older ladies that lived on the road next to her. I wasn't interested in that but pretended to be. I looked at the cloth that I liked and asked, "Do you like this one Nana?"

Author: Victoria E. Kain

"No gal, I don't want anything with no Mickey Mouse on it." She frowned for a moment and said, "Aaaah, this is pretty;" I think I am going to get this if it don't cost too much." She said waiving for the clerk who was standing idle by the rolls of thread staring out the window. It looked as if there were a group of young boys about her age outside that may have been looking at her as well. The girl reluctantly came over to assist us as if she was disturbed that we would interrupt her and she would lose her place in the window from the boys view. We had distracted her from the apparent special attention she was receiving. I thought she may have been dating one of the boys. She looked to be no more than 16 at least, not much older than myself.

Either way the clerk stopped what she was doing, which was nothing, and she faked up a cheerful face and measured the material for Nana and tagged it. "Have a good day y'all!" She said with a southern type drawl. Nana and I politely responded to her and left that section of the store. The girl made a beeline right back to the window. I turned around and it looked like the boys were still stationed right outside the window. So she was able to keep her place. She really wasn't very pretty…I wondered how it was that she had captured that many boys attention. Well, I was too young to think about that anyway. Nana and I walked over to the other section of the store and looked at the dresses for her. When she didn't find anything, she began to look at dresses for me…

I began flipping through the dresses as well and saw one dress that was beautiful. I didn't dare ask Nana to get it for me because Mama would kill me. She pretended not to see me looking at it but glanced over and said,

"Oh, can you fit that dress baby?"

"Yes ma'am I can!" excited that she was entertaining my likes in clothing. "Go try it on gal," "you don't know if it will fit till you do." I ran in the dressing room and put the dress on. It looked beautiful! "What would Patrice and Shellie say when they see me in this dress?" Naomi thought to herself. Peeking out from behind the flimsy curtain hoping Nana had not heard her thinking as if she could read her mind.

I came out of the dressing room and Nana smiled and told me to turn around to model the dress. I did as I was told and even added a curtsey when I stood before her in order to be amusing and get her to smile. It actually worked. Nana then smirked, "Go on and take it off!" Naomi hesitated and had a sad look on her face. She was becoming disappointed. She went back into the dressing room and gave it one last look, thinking she would have to leave the dress in the store. With her heart racing, she came out of the dressing room very slowly and handed the dress to Nana. Nana looked at the dress and then at Naomi. "Come on gal," she said,

"We don't want this dress to get cold before we get to the checkout!" She smiled a big toothy smile and winked at me. I yelled, "Thank you Nana!" "You're welcome baby!"

Author: Victoria E. Kain

Cease To Exist

"Now, don't tell your Mama though, she will have a fit. I will put it in my suitcase until we get back to my house."

"Okay Nana, I won't say anything." I said.

"Not even to Grandpa," she said.

"He forgets sometimes and tells things."

"Yes Ma'am," I said, repeating it again. "I won't say anything."

This was going to be a great day today, I thought, not knowing what was around the corner. We went and got back into the car and put the bags in the back. Nana put the dress in her suitcase just like she said she would. We pulled off and I just sat back smiling and day dreaming, hoping that all went well with leaving with Nana today.

I began to think about when I have to stay in the house while Mama is at work and she does not have the extra money to pay Miss Lucy to sit with me until she gets home. I would stay in the doorway of the locked screen and watch the children play outside while their parents were at work. Sometimes Naomi would entice the kids to come up to the screened porch and talk to Naomi through the door, but there was not much she could do but talk to them and watch them enjoy their childhood like she wished she could.

Today was my day to enjoy and I gloated a little because of what some of the mean children would do when I could never come out to play during school days. If they could see me now! I said, over and over again...I remember how I would try to mesmerize the city kids by telling them all the enchanting stories about my summer vacation out in the country. She would tell such vivid stories it would make them ask if they could come with me sometimes during their summer vacation. I would always say "yes," and tell them that I would ask my parents if they could come, but I knew that would never happen.

This was only a way for me to feel as if I had something to share with other kids and wanted them to sit with me in the doorway to past the time away until mama came home from work. It seemed that daydreaming kept me alive in the moment of my life when everything else around me stood still. It was how I got through the day and dealt with anything that was unpleasant in my life.

At some point I even wished that I did have a brother or sister so I didn't feel so desperate for company. It seemed that I was always alone...But not today. Today was different. I felt alive and full of energy. I was truly happy! Nana had one more stop to make at the mill store to get her kitchen supplies. Grandpa Cody once again circled the building to find just the right parking space to ensure that Nana didn't have to walk far when she came out of the store.

I took that time to reflect on my life while sitting in the back seat waiting for Nana to emerge from the mill store. I always looked beyond what I saw in front of me and vividly remembered things from the past. It didn't seem to matter whose past it was. As long as I knew something about it, I could recall it vividly in my mind and think about it. To pass the time, I thought about the ice cream truck that came by, at the same time I caught sight of the door opening from the store and Nana finally came out.

"Yippee!" I said. "There she is Grandpa Cody!" I yelled. I see her too" he repeated.

"She been in there too long already," he said, mumbling under his breath, making sure he got it all out before Nana opened that car door. He jumped out of the car to open the back of the station wagon to put the groceries in for her.

Regardless of whether he was mad or not, he always was a gentleman to Nana. Nana hesitated for a moment at the back of the station wagon and reached in the bag. She came around to my door and opened it, and handed me a bag of broken crackers.

"Thank you Nana." I said.

"These are my favorites."

"Any cookie is your favorite," Nana said, smiling, as she slowly got in the car complaining about her hip hurting and telling Grandpa that was our last stop.

I hurried and opened the bag of cookies almost losing my breath trying to spy out what kind of cookies I had gotten in the bag. "Oreo's, peanut butter, vanilla crackers, cheese crackers. "Wow, all the good ones!" I thought.

These cookies were the broken crackers that came from the cookie factory that broke while they were on the conveyer belt before they could package. Instead of throwing the cookies away the company decided to package and sells them. That was a smart idea. Most folks couldn't buy the good ones.

You got a taste of all the good cookies that you could not afford to buy for half the price. These were delicious…just when I wished for a glass of milk to go with the cookies, Nana opened her bag and handed me a grape soda…

"Don't get any on the seat, you hear me?"

"I won't," I said, with a huge smile on my face.

I ate the cookies and drank my soda. I thought that nothing could be better than this. Adults never seem to understand that the simple things are the most important to a child. We don't need all the fancy stuff in life. Just love, a few meals and hugs and kisses and we'll be just fine. We were hurrying back to the house so I could pack before we were to leave for Nana's. I hoped the trip would not be cancelled for any reason. We made our way home and Mama met us at the door. Nana tried to hug Mama but she always gave her the side hug. She really didn't want to hug Nana and I never understood why.

Nana told me to go get my bags and put the stuff in the car. Mama stopped me and told Nana, "Well, mom, Naomi can't go with you today because I have some other errands to run and I didn't wash her clothes for the trip. Nana gave mama a hard look. "Peggy, I can wash this child's clothes!"

"Go put them in a bag Naomi." Nana said. Fear stricken, I began to run towards the stairs that led up to my room and the laundry room.

Then Mama made another lame excuse.

"Well, I also made an appointment to get Naomi's hair done as well."

"You know how tangled it will get if it is not washed." Mama said. Nana was furious now,

"Why didn't you tell me that this morning and you could have taken her with you while you were getting yours done?"

"Well, I didn't think she would want to spend that time with me?" Mama said, in a nasty tone.

"You ought to be ashamed of yourself! Nana said.

"You are too old to be lying at this age!"

"Mom, I am not lying," Mama said to Nana.

"Whatever!" Mama shouted back at her.

"You never believe me anyway!"

"When is Naomi coming down to the farm then?" Nana asked in a gruff voice…demanding an answer.

"I will bring her down next Saturday," Mama said, looking like she was afraid now. Nana could be tough when she needed to be and now was the time. I sat down on the steps about to cry because my beautiful euphoric day had just been bombed!

"If you don't bring her down on Saturday morning, I am coming to get her myself!" Nana yelled.

"I mean it Peggy Louise!" she said to Mama, calling her by her whole name denoting a bad situation about to get worse.

"If you don't bring this baby down to the farm, you won't get one penny of me or your daddy's money in the will!"

"I promise you!" Nana chanted with authority. She walked around to the staircase and saw me sitting there with tears in my eyes…

"Don't cry sugar" she said.

"I will see you next Saturday,"

"Besides, it's only a week away and your Mama better have your hair done too.

"It will match that pretty dress I bought you." She whispered, "Our secret!"

I smiled remembering the dress she had bought me in town that was hidden in her suitcase…Nana knew Mama had a bad habit of looking through her bags when she had gone shopping…Nana was slick about that. She knew how nosey Mama was as well.

Nana and Grandpa got in their car and began to pull out of the drive way. Mama stood in the middle of the doorway as if to keep me from waving goodbye. I was sitting on the top step of the stairway and could see directly in the car in the driveway…I waved at Nana and Grandpa and she waved and threw me a kiss…Mama quickly looked back and saw me on the stairs, knowing that the blown kiss was not for her. She threw her hands up at them one last time and slammed the door.

"Naomi, get your clothes in the laundry room so they can be washed…

"Here we go again!" Naomi thought, "Yes ma'am," she said, thinking that if she didn't respond that would be a reason for her to not let me go with Nana next Saturday. I went and got all my clothes and put them in the laundry basket and went back to my room to finish packing for the week. Mama didn't want me to pack that early, so my clothes wouldn't be as wrinkled, but I didn't care. It helped me to be able to visualize being gone from home.

We went through a quiet evening and Mama kept calling me to do little chores. She kept flicking her hair which looked very pretty but it was too oily looking for me. Mama had straight hair and it was blonde. My hair was like daddy's, very curly. It was more with a natural curl and everyone loved touching my hair.

Mama hated it when I was complimented on my hair or even my complexion. I figured I would complement her and maybe it would soften her bad attitude since she and Nana had been arguing about me earlier.

"Your hair looks pretty Mama." I said. Not with much excitement but she responded anyway. It was as if she was hungry for the compliment. Nana did not compliment her hair at all

"Thank you!"

"My hair is so straight but I love it!"

"I don't like the curls that she puts in it like yours. It is too much for me." Mama said. It was a way to put me down about my hair which was like daddies. She always found a way to boast about herself when someone did give her a compliment. Daddy always said my hair was beautiful, but I never paid much attention to it.

Mama made dinner which consisted of hotdogs and chili. Since daddy had been gone overseas, we ate like that all the time. I only got real good meals at Nana's or the baby sitter when I would go there. I didn't care though; the hot dogs were good to me. Mama didn't say anything to me while we ate; she just kept looking at me looking at my food. She finally asked what we did in town. I responded quickly with a flat "Nothing!"

"Stop lying," Mama said, as if she wanted to call me a liar like Nana had called her earlier.

I wanted to say that I got the lying from her but remembered I still wanted to go to Nana's. Finally I spoke,

"We went to the mill store for flour, corn meal, butter, eggs and paprika. "Where else did you go?"

"Nana got me a bag of the broken crackers," I liked...

"You like anything someone gives you." I sat quietly and thought, "Well, who wouldn't.

Author: Victoria E. Kain

"Anything else?"

I said. "No!" "Nothing."

It was as if she wanted to see if I would tell her everything we did. She wanted to hold something over Nana's head if I told her anything we talked about. I would never tell something if Nana asked me not too. "Nope..." that's all I said. I was happy that I could have my own secrets from mama like she had from daddy and me.

"Well, you need to go to bed early tonight, I have company coming over." "Ok," I said. I didn't know who was coming over but really didn't care. Since daddy was gone she often had company on the weekends. Just when I was finishing up dinner, the phone rang. Finally it was daddy! He was calling long distance...Mama answered in her sweetest voice.

"Well, well, look at what the cat drug in," she said.

"How are you?"

"Do you miss me?" she asked daddy, as she began to usher me upstairs and whisper...

"I'll give you your dessert later." Naomi was fine with that. She was accustomed to being shooed away like an annoying gnat when her daddy called. She obediently ran upstairs and got ready for bed.

"There she goes again," Naomi thought, lying to keep daddy from speaking to me!"

Cease To Exist

I could never understand why I was not to be loved by my own father. I was afraid to ask the question knowing that Mama would be mad at me and I would never go to Nana's again if she thought I told Nana anything of what goes on here in the house when daddy was away. Mama talked to daddy for a few minutes and then I heard her ask him,

"Who is that in the background David?" Momma kept talking and apparently it was a women close by him. And then momma said, "Well, she sounds like she is awful close to you!" Daddy must have responded to mama's statement.

"Oh, really, it's someone else's lady…?" Mama said.

"Humph, well, I'll just bet you have a lady of your own there as well and this little cheap call is to soothe your conscious about what you are about to do or have already done!" Then the yelling began. He must have asked to speak to me and she went off, "SHE IS ASLEEP!!!" She is asleep!!!"

"You don't need to talk to her anyway because the truth is, SHE DOESN'T BELONG TO YOU!!!"

"Why don't you get someone there pregnant and you can have what you really want from a woman, which is a curly headed child of your own!!!!" Mama yelled so loud it startled me. I quietly closed my bedroom door not knowing what to think about what she had just said. "Is this true?" I mouthed the words looking up against the wall as if it could tell me the answer I needed to hear.

"If he is not my daddy, then who is?" I thought

"Is it the guy that was here last week, or the one that is coming this weekend?" Now I was really confused… I didn't know what to think and hurried to get in bed knowing Mama was going to come upstairs to check and see if I was there. Sure enough, she came upstairs and peeked in… I pretended to be asleep. She knew I wasn't, but dared not ask if I heard anything. She simply closed the door like she does the lid to the dirty clothes basket and went back down stairs.

This may be why she never wanted me to talk to daddy. I don't know what to do now. When you think someone loves you and you find out they don't, what are you supposed to think? I lay there for a while and finally I heard the doorbell ring. I heard voices and laughter coming from downstairs.

Since she had promised me cake for dessert, I figured I would sneak down and get a piece myself. Once I got down to the bottom of the stairs, I heard giggling in the den. I heard a man's voice and at first thought it was daddy but I hesitated, realizing she had just spoken to him and fought with him on the phone. Who was this person with Mama? I opened the fridge and took out the cake plate. Just as I began to bag the cake up and put it back, I reached for the milk and a strange man stepped from around the fridge. I dropped the milk and some spilled on the floor. He grabbed it before it could all spill out and I stood there frozen in my tracks.

Cease To Exist

He was tall and had a deep tan. He had hazel eyes and a thick mustache…not like daddy's thin one. He had huge hands and feet like he could have been a ball player, but I was afraid to speak. Mama heard the container fall and asked, "Vincent, what was that?" Vincent put his finger up to his mouth in the hush mode to silence me and yelled,

"I dropped the milk baby," I am getting it up now so don't worry your pretty little head about it." Vincent said to mama, like he was the owner of the house.

"Alright now," Mama said.

"Hurry and come back sweetie!" She announced in a sultry voice. I knew what that voice was because I had heard her use it on daddy when she wanted something. Was this my mother speaking so nicely to this man after she had talked to my daddy or whoever's dad he is, like a dog? I thought.

The man looked at me and whispered,

"You must be Naomi?"

I gave a reluctant but affirmative nod to the stranger. He then said, "Well, I am Vincent as you now know and this will be our secret, okay!" I nodded once again as if I were mute just staring at him to make sure his hands never touched my cake. Lord only knows where they had been. He gave me the slice of cake on a paper towel and gave me a glass of milk. "Run on upstairs before your mom decides to come out of the den." He whispered and then he winked at me and I took off like a bullet!!!

"Oh, my goodness", I thought.

Author: Victoria E. Kain

"He was very handsome!" Naomi quickly looked behind her to see if he was behind her as if he could hear what she was thinking. She wondered who else was downstairs with Mama…She got to her room and closed the door and locked it. She was a smart girl and was taking no more chances of someone creeping upstairs if Mama were to leave them in the house all night. It was kind of scary, but I didn't trust anyone other than the man I called daddy and Grandpapa Cody. Even though the stranger in the house appeared harmless, I was not taking any chances.

I knew for sure I couldn't win in a fight with him if I tried, so I remembered what daddy always said, "Any unidentified fish is a shark!" I was always to be cautious if I didn't know you or your intentions. Naomi locked her bedroom door and pushed her toy chest filled with all the stuff in her room from years ago. It was a bit heavy, but I could slide it over just enough to cover the door opening. Anyone trying to get in would make enough noise to wake me up and then I could get my baseball bat which was down under the side of my bed just in case. I had my attack mode ready if needed. I forgot about the stranger for a minute and ate my cake and wondered what else Mama fought about with daddy on the phone earlier. This had been going on every time daddy was away. Ever since I was little, I remember the arguments and Mama telling me when I was old enough to sleep alone, to go in my room and don't come down stairs.

Cease To Exist

When I was seven and daddy went to Columbia, she changed the locks on my bedroom door to a key lock on the outside. I never knew why she would change the lock and put a regular one back on the door before daddy came home.

I was beginning to put some pieces together, but was a bit concerned about what I heard earlier and now what I had seen downstairs. 'Why was this other man downstairs in daddy's house?' Naomi thought, as she quickly ate the icing off the red velvet cake. "Umm, this cake is good!" She said, busying herself with eating all of it bite by bite. The neighbor had made this cake for Mama and me but I didn't get much of it. I never did. She always ate everything. Especially when daddy was away. It seemed that she always had a weight problem, but it was because she was always eating when he was away, like she was nervous or something.

Tonight, I was savoring the piece I had though. All the while wondering what was happening to Mama. I am still young but I knew more than Mama gave me credit for understanding. I really didn't care, but I wanted to know if daddy was really my daddy or not. Naomi stopped for a moment and lamented,

"First things first," I thought, as if to rationalize on what I would stand to gain out of this situation.

'I want to go home out to Nana's for the summer…once I get there, everything will be alright.' I know it will, I said.

Author: Victoria E. Kain

Cease To Exist

Who were these people that mama was entertaining down stairs? How many were there? The strange thing was that I only heard male voices. Her friend Deanna was not here at the house this night because I would recognize her voice. She was very loud and would always come up and give me candy through the door when mom was busy or not watching her. Maybe these are just old friends of Mama's and I need to forget about it. It was hard to forget about this because daddy was always gone and mama always had people over.

I knew they played cards a lot but I was never allowed downstairs after dark so I don't know what else may have been happening down there. Finally Naomi decided to drink her milk and got up to brush her teeth and jumped back in bed. She carefully placed her dolls on the other side of the bed with her for company. She stopped thinking about Mama, her friends, her locked door or the baseball bat that was on the floor by her bed for protection. She even blocked out the sound of the children that were outside playing jump rope in the street in front of their houses.

She never got to do anything like that. She always had to stay in her room that looked like the American flag. Finally she stopped wondering what was going on downstairs. She did what all twelve year olds did after they ate anything sweet… she fell fast asleep full of cake and milk only to be haunted again by her bad dreams that she had never told anyone else about.

~CHAPTER 3 ~

The Summer That Saved Me

The weekend went by fast and Monday and Tuesday was a blur. Wednesday and Thursday was even more blurred, then, it was finally Friday. Mama looked sheepish all week and was quiet. She had a strange look on her face as if she suspected that I knew something but she was afraid to ask me. On Friday I had to stay with the baby sitter because Mama had something she had to do after work. She normally picked me up at 3:30, but would come at 5:30 instead. The baby sitter was almost 80 years old. It was as if people took their kids over there to watch her instead of being watched. Everyone in the neighborhood did this as a way to help her with money. They paid a small amount and it helped Ms. Lucy get her medication. I watched the smaller kids while Ms. Lucy slept and farted in her sleep.

The kids would make fun of her then try to steal candy from her apron pocket when she took off her glasses because she couldn't see who it was. She used the candy to bribe the kids to do things for her like find her glasses and sweep the floor. I called it child slavery. Either way, she was really a sweet old lady. Mama came to get me at 5:30 on the nose and Ms. Lucy woke up right before she knocked on the door. She pretended like she was wide awake and hurried the kids around to show she had earned her money.

Author: Victoria E. Kain

I was watching TV with all the fuzz on it. Of course she didn't have a flat screen. Mama walked in like the police, looking around as if she was searching for drugs or something.

"Get your things Naomi." She said abruptly, as if I was under arrest and bail less.

"Yes ma'am," I responded in a robotic voice. I was actually ready to go when she came in. She asked Ms. Lucy the same question.

"Was Naomi a good girl", she said

"Oh, Naomi, never gives me any trouble, it's all these other little devils around here that are bad...she is always good", Ms. Lucy said, smiling a big toothless smile. I believe the kids had moved her teeth out of the jar they were in as a joke when she went to the bathroom.

"Well, I know you still have to watch her too" Mama said, as if not to accept that I could be as good as Ms. Lucy said I was. Mama always seemed to want to think the worst of me.

"Well, she was good! Ms. Lucy snapped back, again refuting what Mama had said. She reminded me of Nana when she snapped at mama like that. It was as if the older women knew what mama was about and they responded in kind to her snide remarks about me. Mama gave her a long stare but she didn't role her eyes only out of respect for Ms. Lucy. Mama then reached in her purse and pulled out a twenty dollar bill and put it in Ms. Lucy's pocket and said, thank you to her.

Ms. Lucy accepted the money and took it out of the pocket where mama put it and stuck it in her other apron pocket that had what appeared to be hundreds of dollars from all the children's mothers who had already picked up their children.

Mama just looked at her and when she was out of sight of Ms. Lucy, she rolled her eyes at her. Mama really should have given the twenty dollars to me because Ms. Lucy slept the whole time I was there and I actually watched the kids.

I really didn't mind though. We picked up my things and walked out the door. I hurried to the back seat because Mama never let me sit in the front with her. She said I was too young to sit up there with adults. I didn't care and didn't understand "what adults" she was talking about, I just got in.

"Why are you in such a hurry?" Mama asked.

"I am ready to go!" Naomi said, hurrying in the car.

"I got lots of packing to do for my trip tomorrow!" I snapped back, as if to say, "good riddance!"

Mama started up the engine and let the windows down in the back only. It was hotter than all get out and I didn't want my hair to blow with all the wind coming into the back seat. I think she did that on purpose because my hair was very curly.

Anytime she thought I was being a smart mouth, she would do little things like that to me. "Can you let the window up Mama," I asked, "No," she snapped back as if she was glad to turn down any request that I made of her.

"I want to save gas."

"You want to get to Nana's tomorrow don't you?" She asked.

"Yes ma'am," I said, grimacing behind her seat.

"Well, this gas has to take you there and pick you back up!" like she wasn't going anywhere while I was gone. Please! I thought.

I didn't say anything else and she knew I was mad. I wanted to tell her to ask "Vincent" for the money. He didn't seem to mind buying her more milk that was spilled. But, I knew if I had said that to Mama, she would have thrown me out of the car and run over me. Finally about half way home she let the window up and turned on the air like this was some kind of treat or reprieve for the punishment she heaped on me in all that heat. The thing was, she was hot too and I know how she loved it colder than I did. I guess I had been pardoned for getting in the car. She was the one who had to spend the money getting my hair done so I really didn't care, but I said nothing…not even thank you. I just let my curly locks blow in the wind and she could see me in her rear view mirror.

At this age, most of my friends would be sassing their parents back and forth, but I just say nothing to keep myself out of trouble. I wasn't worried about anything. I knew I had only tonight to sleep in the house with Mama and whoever would be with her and then I would be off to Nana's and would see my friends Shellie and Patrice for the whole summer.

Cease To Exist

We got home and Mama cooked a light dinner and we ate quietly like we always do. I wasn't feeling very hungry so I hurried to finish my meal and decided to pack all my things for the months I would be gone to Nana's. I put my bags by my door. It was Friday night and all the girls in the neighborhood had parties they were going to at school mates houses, but I never got to go anywhere like that.

I busied myself with cleaning the dishes and thought about what I would take with me to Nana's for the summer. I use to put my suitcase downstairs but Mama would take certain outfits out so I stopped putting it downstairs. Besides, I am twelve now and should be able to make some decision on my own, or so I thought. Mama treated me like an infant. She said I should turn in early, so after cleaning the dishes I went straight to my room. I was accustomed to that but knew I was not going to sleep right away. I still couldn't understand why I always had to go to bed early on Friday nights? I thought. It may have been because Mama had her friends over and I was not allowed to go out of my room when she had company.

After watching TV and writing a letter to daddy and hiding it under my mattress, a few hours went by and I heard the doorbell ring downstairs. Mama invited someone in and there was laughing and I heard different voices again.

I was really tired of having to be a hostage in my room when the big T.V. was in the den. Ever since I could remember, if Mama said stay in your room, that's where I stayed. But tonight, I was not going to go without my dessert regardless of who was here!

Author: Victoria E. Kain

Mama had told me I could have cake every Friday or Saturday as a treat for the weekend and I was going to have cake again tonight. I felt that this was her way of paying me for my silence, but I knew that at some point, cake was not going to keep me quiet. I decided once again to sneak downstairs regardless of what Mama had told me.

You would think I could have some leniency since I was almost a teenager. Other girls were already dating guys at school, not that I wanted to, but here I was still going to a baby sitter for crying out loud. I guess that was a good thing on mama's part if I have to give her credit for caring about me at all. I quietly opened the door making sure no one could hear or see me. The house was big enough to conceal me and I was on the second floor down the hall. By the time I got to the staircase, I tiptoed down the steps until I could see into the den but no one could see me. The kitchen was on the other end of the first floor so I had two ways to escape in case someone came out of the den. I just had to be really fast.

I went down the last set of stairs and again went to the fridge…having experienced seeing a man come out of the den the last time, I didn't expect to see anyone else on this trip. I reached into the fridge to get the cake out and some milk and I heard someone coming into the kitchen. I did not have time to put the milk back and dropped it on the floor, again! Thinking it was Mama, I panicked! I bent down to pick up the milk carton. This time to my surprise, it was another man!!!

'What is going on here, I thought?' Frozen in my tracks, I was really scared now.

'What is Mama doing with these different men in the house while daddy is gone?' I thought. What could she be thinking? This is not good! Again, this man gives me the shush finger and asks me to quietly go back upstairs.

He takes the carton out of my hand and this time the man stares me deep into my eyes and this one touched my hair. I recoiled like a snake ready to strike and backed up quickly as the hair stood up on my arms like it would on a dogs back when he was getting angry.

"You are off limits" he said to me, giving me a sinister look and raising an eyebrow. I knew he was not like the other man. I was scared now and mad all at the same time. This time I knocked the container of milk to the floor from his hand and there was a louder noise than when it had accidentally fell the first time. The man was mortified! He didn't know what to do. Mama yelled,

"What in heaven's name was that Frank?" Mama asked the man.

"I accidentally dropped the milk bottle," he quickly responded, trying to hurry and clean up the mess I'd made before she possibly walked in. I enjoyed seeing him scramble knowing he had no business being here.

He quickly recanted.

"Sorry about that!"

"I will buy you two more darling."

"But it's all cleaned up now." He said, in a rushed voice trying to reassure her that she didn't need to come out of the den.

"Okay! She said in her nicest voice…as in, "don't let me see anything on that floor when I come through there again." I didn't know who that voice was because mama never talked to anyone that nice. She was a totally different person when these men were around. I wondered why she was nicer to these men than she was to daddy…time would answer all of those questions I had about what was actually going on in my life.

Her response to him was the same one she would give me if I had done something she wanted me to fix. That voice meant, it better be done, or else! Well, at least I knew she was in control of the person because he appeared truly shaken by the mishap. He had a scowl on his face now like he was mad at me for doing what I did. I didn't care anymore. I was sick of coming into my daddy's kitchen or whoever's daddy he really was and seeing these different men in our fridge where we kept our food!

They simply had no right! I was glad I was leaving in the morning so these people could have the house. I wondered, how many had been here in the house over these years. Usually I was told to stay in my room on Friday nights. I knew I was growing up now because I was beginning to feel different about information that was kept from me. This was crazy! I ran back upstairs and went to my room and locked my door. I was so furious that I searched for the number to call daddy. I had really had it! Were my hormones already kicking in for my teenage years? If so, I felt that it was going to be very tough for me going forward. I was tired of feeling afraid and not having any fun.

Cease To Exist

I was sick of Mama telling daddy I was asleep or in my room when he was overseas and would call. She would never let me talk to him and if I did, it was only for seconds and she'd snatch the phone as soon as she saw me laughing or enjoying hearing his voice.

It was as if I were the other woman or something. I didn't understand it at all. Why wouldn't she let me talk to him just like she did? After all, he was my daddy! Actually, I remembered mama's conversation and didn't know if he was my daddy. Naomi stopped thinking and retracted her thoughts with a sigh.

"Well, maybe he is not my daddy as Mama said." Naomi was really angry now and began to look for her daddy's number to call him.

"Dang," it seemed like I am always the last one to know anything around here," She said. Finally finding the number written on the back of her lamp, she now remembered hiding it there when her mama was mad with her daddy and came into her room and ripped it apart like she was looking for drugs or something one day. She sighed, a sigh of relief. She had hidden it in another place so that her Mama wouldn't know that she had it at all. It was a shame I had to hide stuff from her like that, but maybe her conversation with her daddy about her not being his child explained it all. If this were true, what was she going to do with her? Everyone seemed to get to do what they want to do but me!!!

"I'm not taking it anymore!!! I said.

Author: Victoria E. Kain

Seeing a different man in the house now two weekends in a row really frightened me. I wondered how many more had been in the house before while I was sleeping. I knew if I didn't tell someone I would burst. Naomi took the number and picked up the phone to call her daddy.

She reasoned that she would call him daddy until she heard it directly from him that he wasn't her father at all. She hoped he would answer and be glad to hear from her but knew it was late where she was but early for him overseas. She had looked up the time zone on the map with my tablet and the time would have been about 6am in the morning. She knew he would be up now because they got up at 5am. The phone rang and rang and rang. She hoped her Mama would not pick up the phone, because sometimes the phone would have a low ringing tone in another room if someone was on it upstairs.

She dismissed the thought and figured her mama was busy anyway and wouldn't pay much attention to the phone. She probably was scared thinking daddy might call. Naomi was surprised she was able to get a dial tone. She focused on the ringing number still.

"If he doesn't pick up, I thought, I'll just talk to Nana when I get there tomorrow. She won't tell Mama but she will find out what is going on. I'm also going to tell her about the dreams I've been having and the headaches too. The phone rang one more time and broke Naomi's daydreaming. She figured if he didn't pick up on this next ring she would hang up. Finally she heard his voice, "Capt. Kilpatrick"

"Daddy, it's me, Naomi!"

"Oh, my word!"

"Sweetie, how are you?" her daddy asked in a loving fatherly voice. It was the voice she had missed so much.

"I am fine daddy, how are you?" I said, smiling harder than I thought I ever could. It was not often she felt this good.

"I'm okay sweetie!" he said.

"I miss you daddy." Naomi said, falling back on the pillow feeling that everything was okay now that she was talking to her dad. It all felt so right that she could talk to him even if her heart was broken by what her mama had said about him not being her father. She only hated that her mother never permitted her to speak to him when he was away, which was always. She would savor the moment because she knew it wouldn't last long and her mama would start the next day off with a negative attitude about something.

"I've missed you too darling."

"But guess what?" Daddy said.

"What, daddy?" Naomi asked.

"You won't have to miss me much longer!"

"Really?" Naomi asked, confused, knowing he had six months left overseas. Grinning and listening at the door to make sure Mama hadn't tiptoed upstairs to see if she was sleeping, she asked another question…

"Why won't I have to miss you any longer, it's not time for you to come home…?"

"Well, my orders were changed and I am being released early from duty here. I am in a cab right now on my way to the house."

Naomi was feeling numb not knowing how to respond to the new information. Everything was going through her head all at once. She was happy and then when she realized what was happening in the house, she was sad. Her daddy continued to talk.

"I left yesterday to get home before you left for Nana's tomorrow and I wanted to surprise your mom…" but when I called her earlier today, she started an argument about the folk that were here at the barracks a week ago who were talking in the background. I just didn't tell her I had gotten my duty changed and would be coming home. You know how suspicious your Mama is? He said.

"I know daddy! I am glad you are coming home now! Naomi was very happy her daddy was finally coming home, but remembered why she had called him and panicked…

"Oh, my God, Daddy's coming home tonight?" Someone is going to get hurt…I just know it!

"What made you call me baby? Her daddy asked, in an authoritative voice.

"Is everything okay with you and your mother?" daddy said, demanding an answer.

"Everything is fine daddy," Naomi lied, making a face over the phone.

"Other than you missed me huh?" He said.

"Well, I just missed you, that's all" knowing I was lying. That was not the only reason she had called him. I wanted to tell on Mama but she was about to tell on herself. I didn't know what to say when daddy asked the next question, I felt like I couldn't even be happy to see my daddy or whoever he was, under these circumstances.

"Where is your mother?"

"Uhhh, she is in the Den." I hurriedly said ending that part of the conversation.

"I came to my room after dinner to get some sleep before tomorrow Daddy." "You know I'm going to Nana's right?" I asked.

"Yes baby! I really have missed you. Daddy said again, as if to reassure me. It was music to my ears because Mama never said she missed me even when I would come back from Nana's.

Did your Mama give you the money I sent you for your school trip this year?"

"What money daddy, I didn't get any. I didn't go." Naomi said.

"Your mother didn't give you the two hundred dollars I sent for your trip?

"No daddy, I didn't go on the trip, Mama said we didn't have the money."

"I knew Mama was lying!" Naomi thought.

Daddy began swearing for a moment and then remembered he was in a cab and I was a kid on the phone.

"Never mind, I will address that later with your mother." "Maybe something came up that she didn't tell me about." Trying to reassure himself that she had not done with the money what he knew she had, and he did not want to let me hear him thinking badly of her. After all, he did love Mama even if it appeared that she did not love him.

"Well, I am about 25 minutes away from the house now pumpkin, so don't tell her, I want to see the surprised look on her face when I walk in."

"Aaaah, okay daddy," I said, knowing that the look of surprise will be on daddy's face when he sees this strange man in his house. Unless Mama can get him out quickly, this will be a disaster!

"Okay, this call will be our secret!" Daddy said.

"What is going on?" I thought.

"This is the third time a man has told me to keep a secret this week!"

"Is this normal? Naomi thought.

"I am only twelve years old, but good grief does everyone keep secrets!"

"Do all men tell females to keep secrets and why do they have to have so many of them when some of this stuff is little things like spilled milk and a phone call."

"What should I do now?" She thought, as she hurried to get back in bed as if this would protect her. Naomi always sent up a quick prayer when she didn't know what else to do.

"Lord please don't let Mama get hurt or daddy for that matter.

"On the other hand, the other guy should get some kind of punishment" but I will leave it up to you." "Amen." She said.

Naomi was still nervous as she tried to figure out what to do.

"Should I go and tell Mama, Daddy is on his way?"

"No" she thought,

"Then, I would have to explain how I knew he was on the way and she didn't hear the phone ring." She would surely blame me and then daddy would have to console me and that would be a fight as well....I am in a giant pickle...I don't know if I want to be an adult Naomi said....

"Should I tell daddy that mama has company?"

"No," she said.

"I can't do that either because he is sure to want to leave Mama if she lies to him, then I won't ever see daddy again," she frantically thought. Her young mind was completely confused now.

"I don't know what to do!" Naomi thought, tugging at her bangs and raking them all the way back off of her face over and over again. The day before my vacation is turning into a disaster again!" She thought, feeling a headache coming on as she lay across her bed, burying her head in her pillow, wanting to scream but knowing her Mama would hear her.

"If only Mama had let me go with Nana, I wouldn't even have seen this!" She angrily whispered in a hushed tone. I would have seen daddy when he came to Nana's tomorrow and that would be it!!! I hate growing up and understanding adult things. Naomi prayed that no one got hurt tonight.

Before her prayers were finished, she heard her daddy walk in the door down stairs.

"Peggy, where are you?" Daddy called for Mama in a sweet voice. Like a newlywed husband waiting to see his lovely bride.

"I am home baby! He said.

Hearing daddy's voice, I instinctively started to run downstairs to greet him but froze before I could get midway the steps realizing what I might walk into. Daddy had already made his way into the den looking for mama.

He would soon find her with her friend .... I stood frozen...my heart racing, now praying again to be safe. All I heard from that point forward was screaming, and yelling and furniture crashing against the walls!

"What is this?" daddy asked. Not waiting for mama to answer. Now sending out more commands.

"Private!!!...what are you doing here in my house?" Daddy growled, announcing the man's rank showing his authority over him.

"Peggy, you'd better explain this situation fast and it better make sense to me!!!" Daddy said, in a gruff voice which was getting louder each time he spoke to mama or the man in his house. Mama was trying to explain but she couldn't. I came down a few more steps and could see into the den and daddy was walking towards the man with urgency and his fist drawn back. They couldn't see me, but I could see that Mama had on her slip.

"Why was mama in her slip?" I thought. I thought they only played cards. That's what she told me! Mama looked over as if instinct told her I was there and saw me before I could duck back up the steps...

"Naomi!" She yelled at the top of her voice. "Go back upstairs and stay there!" Mama screamed! DON'T COME OUT TILL I CALL YOU!!! I mean it or you will be in big trouble!!!

"No, Peggy," Daddy screamed, as he struck the man with one hand. "My child will NOT be in trouble ever again!!!" You have abused her and me enough!

"But you, on the other hand are the one that's in trouble!!! He screamed! Real trouble!

Daddy was yelling and striking the man who was trying to fight back. Daddy was bigger and stronger and the man was now cowering on the floor trying to protect himself from the massive blows daddy was giving him. Mama was crying…I had never seen her cry like that before. It was the first time I had seen her in a vulnerable position and realized that she was afraid of daddy even though she always talked to him like she wasn't. She realized that he was mad and that she had been wrong. There was a lot of noise in the house. The man was trying to explain his relationship with Mama and get out of daddy's way, all at the same time. Daddy wasn't hearing any of that. I heard a lot of things being broken and Mama was screaming telling daddy,

"It's not what you think!!! She said, still crying and screaming!

"It's not what you think!!!" She now is bursting into more and more unstoppable tears.

"What is it then!" daddy yelled?

"You better tell me something better than this Peggy!"

"You have no idea what I am thinking right now!"

I closed the door and locked it after that. I hoped the neighbors couldn't hear all this madness and call the police so I got under the bed. I began to cry and just laid there covering my ears. "What had I done?"

"Did I really cause this bad thing to happen?" It doesn't matter…I thought. It's over now anyway. Daddy will probably kill the man and go to prison.

Mama will run off with someone else and leave me for the wolves I guess.

I didn't know what to think….will I ever be happy and have a normal family again? Did I ever have a life in the first place? What if this is not my daddy? Then what? The thoughts kept flooding my head. I went and put my ear plugs in and hid in my closet where I slept in the fetal position all night with my dolls. That night I found comfort in the darkness of my closet floor. It felt strangely familiar.

The next morning came quickly as I slowly exited my darkened safe haven and removed my barricades from the door way. I looked over on the floor and saw an envelope on the floor in front of my door. It was still half way in the hallway and in my room like it was pushed under in a hurry. I wondered what it was. In an examination of the envelope, it was a note from Mama. I was scared to open it and peaked downstairs first to see if the coast was clear. I finally got the courage to look in the rooms upstairs to make sure no one was up there with me and when I saw that there was no one there but me, I sat on the steps and read the note.

The Note:

Cease To Exist

Naomi, I don't know if you heard everything last night with me and your daddy. His coming home early created a problem you don't understand. We had a big fight and I am going away for a while because daddy and I are not getting along. He insists that you will stay with him for reasons he will tell you about soon. I thought it would be best if you stay with him as well.

There are things I cannot say to you because I know you are my child, but I have feelings that do not coincide with those feelings of a mother. I believe I had you for all the wrong reasons, but did not know how to deal with my decision. You will still go to Nana's for the summer as planned. I will let you know where I am much later so you can come visit me if you would like some times in the future. I want you to know that I care for you although it may not have seemed like it sometimes. I don't want you to make the mistakes I made so be careful about who you marry in life. I can say now that I didn't give you the love you deserved but maybe your daddy can. As you grow up you will understand life more when you have your own children. I know you are a smart girl so stay in school. I will try to keep in touch.   *Mama*

Tears welled up in my eyes and I threw the note down and ran downstairs hoping that daddy hadn't left me too. What happened last night…I wondered? I got to the bottom of the stairs and looked around and the house and it was a wreck! The den had broken lamps and tables and glass was everywhere. I looked in the closet and put on a pair of mamas old house slippers so as not to get my feet cut with all the glass. The flat screen was flat on the floor and there were alcohol bottles still unopened. The spare bedroom looked as if someone had been in it, and there was a man's shoe on the floor but I knew it wasn't Daddy's. The covers were thrown about on the floor like someone had been struggling in there.

I slowly walked over to Jared's bedroom which was always locked, but was open today. I saw another man's shoe on the floor beside the bed tossed aside like the wearer had left in a hurry. Then I saw daddy lying on the bed.

Daddy woke up abruptly as if her were at war.

"Naomi?" he whispered, in a tired deep voice… squinting his bloodshot eyes like he wasn't sure who I was.

"Yes daddy!"

"Come on in here baby!"

I went into the room and he sat up on the side of the bed fully clothed in his military uniform. His bag was over in the corner like he had just arrived.

"Let me look at you!" he said in a whisper, almost moved to tears. It was the look of a fathers love in his eyes that I will never forget. You know that look when someone is happy to see you. There is something about how they hold you in their vision for a while and a pleasant calm comes over them as they reach to hug you. He looked as if he couldn't believe how I had grown up. I had been hidden away from him for so long, right under his nose. His look was as if he was resolved never to let it happen again.

"You are all grown up!" he said.

He hugged me very tightly.

"I missed you so much darling."

"You are all I have now."

"Daddy, I missed you too."

"Where did Mama go?" Naomi asked, with tears in her eyes.

"She left us baby!"

"But, why daddy?" Bursting into a floodgate of tears, now soaking her clean bed shirt.

"She only had friends over sometimes!" she said. Hoping he'd believe her.

"That's what she told me." Naomi was still crying trying to get her daddy to think differently about the situation.

"Why did she have to leave daddy?"

"It was for the best honey." He dad responded.

I'll tell you all about this when we get you something to eat. It looks like you have lost weight since I was away…was your Mama feeding you?

"Yes daddy, she was." Daddy knew I was lying.

"I didn't eat much so we didn't have to spend much money on food."

"I gave your Mama plenty of money for groceries and all I saw in the fridge was milk and snacks." A frown had appeared on his face and he was now biting his lips.

"Well, things are going to change for us now honey. I promise. I will never leave you."

"Nothing is going to stop you from your summer vacation though!"

"As a matter of fact, when we get to Nana's, we are all going out to eat at that place in town that you like! How about that? Still teary eyed, I mustered up a smile and leaned on his shoulder and closed my eyes.

"That would be nice daddy." I would like that. He hugged me again and then ushered me upstairs to get changed so we could go out and get breakfast. Daddy called our neighbor who had a cleaning service and asked them to come over to clean up the mess that was made in the house. I knew that daddy would take care of everything and as I walked back upstairs I breathed a sigh of relief almost. It was as if someone had broken a spell and a heavy weight was lifted off me. Even though I was sad that Mama had left, I felt that I could rest now. Daddy was home and it was just the two of us. No more cloak and dagger from Mama trying to keep us apart.

I wanted to find the right time to ask him if he was my real daddy or not. I just didn't know if this was the right time. I knew I still needed to belong somewhere, and had to know the truth. I am old enough to understand what it means not to belong to someone. I still want to know! My life has to get better than it was. Finally daddy changed into civilian clothes and shaved and we walked out of the front door to get in the car to go out for breakfast. It felt different walking out of the door with daddy than it did with mama. I got ready to get in the back seat and daddy stopped me.

"Why are you getting in the back seat Naomi? You don't want to sit in the front with me?" Daddy asked, with a puzzled look of dejection on his face.

"Mama never let me sit in the front with her." I said quietly.

"Oh, well you are to sit up here with me from now on Kiddo!" He said. "There are no safety reasons why you can't. You are twelve and past the weight requirement."

"Get on up here! He smiled a reassuring smile as if things would be different now. I jumped in the front seat now feeling like I was not a little kid anymore but becoming a young lady. It was as if I had gone back in time and was experiencing some things that I had missed in life. I buckled up and smiled at daddy as he looked over his shoulder and backed out of the driveway. I stared at daddy for a moment and looked at myself in the mirror to see if I thought I looked like him and he saw me doing this.

"What are you doing pumpkin?" Daddy asked.

Scared, thinking he would be mad if I asked the question about him being my daddy and not wanting to rat Mama out, I said, "nothing daddy."

"Now you know that's a fib Naomi, you don't have to be afraid to tell me the truth." He gently said. It was either now or never to get this out in the open. I was scared but needed to know the truth and decided to let it all fly.

"Well, the last time you called and talked to Mama, she told you that you should go get a kid of your own because I am not your kid." Naomi was shaking now, scared that she would lose the last parent she thought she had.

Kids in the neighborhood had at least one parent and now she might not have anyone.

Daddy was very quiet for a moment…

"Pumpkin, is that what you think?"

"I don't know daddy, I mean… Mama said…there was silence and Daddy stopped me mid-sentence.

"You are old enough to know some truths now Naomi. I hoped never to have to tell you this, but you should know the truth."

"Your mother and I had this conversation over 12 years ago after you were born."

"She wasn't sure if I was your father because she was seeing someone else when I met her and began dating."

"I fell in love with her and then she told me she was pregnant with you. She was not sure if you were mine, so she assumed that you weren't. I didn't know if she accepted my marriage proposal because she was pregnant and thought that the man she had just broken up with wouldn't have believed that you belonged to him, so she married me. I was never sure she really loved me, but I knew I loved you both. I've wondered that during our entire marriage. I never told this to her until last night when I came home but I did a paternity test on you to ensure that you were mine when you were only 6 months old."

"I knew I loved you regardless, but because I wasn't sure if your mother was in love with me since she already had your brothers, I just had to be sure for myself. You are mine 100%! He said with a big smile. However, what your mother has shown since then showed that she didn't really love me."

"Naomi, she treated you different because she didn't realize that you were mine and she didn't want me getting close to you thinking that one day the man she thought was your father would come back to take you away from us. She also was in love with the other man and had not let go of him. I married her because I loved her and I knew you were my child. I tried to make a family and a home for all of us regardless of what she had done."

"She really wasted a lot of her time and mine." He said, in a low tone as he turned on the radio as if to drown out his feelings for what he felt for mama. I loved your mother Naomi, but realize she really wanted to be on her own but she had you which kept her from doing that." "It didn't mean she didn't love you," he added as a way to make me feel better, but it didn't.

"That's why she never went anywhere with me and was too selfish to let you go anywhere with me."

"Last night was just the culmination of years of faking a relationship for the wrong reasons and making your little life miserable."

"I am sorry for doing this to you."

"I promise you I will make it up if it is the last thing I do. You have always been a good child and have not been given the love you deserve by both your parents and all that changes right now!" Naomi smiled very hard and was relieved at the same time! She had stopped listening when she heard her daddy say she was 100% his. This is my daddy! It really is, and now I don't have to be afraid that no one will be here for me. Daddy took me out to breakfast that morning and then we were on our way to Nana's house. I felt sorry for Mama but felt good that I could be free to talk to daddy any time I wanted.

How would it feel to be free with Nana? No more hiding things she does for me and tip toeing around mama when all I wanted to do was be happy and love her and be loved.

I hoped that things would be better for Mama and they could get back together, but I felt it wouldn't happen in my life time. In this wonderfully soothing conversation, daddy also told me that mama decided to leave when he told her that he had done the paternity test. He knew when she insinuated that I was not his child over the phone earlier, it was time to tell her. He also said he knew then that she really did not love him. He squelched all my fears of me having to feel responsible for last night's events also. He said, "even if this hadn't happened with the man being here with your mama, I was going to tell her the truth about you and let her go free if she wanted to." I was tired of living a lie myself about what I knew she felt for me. But, when she realized that you were my child, your Mama had the look of defeat on her face. Then she said to me,

"Well, it's done, I can take my leave now."

"You have what you want and the two of you can have each other."

It was as if she felt she would have to compete for his love for me but she really would not have to do that because daddy loved Mama very much, she just didn't love herself. She did not have to worry about him leaving me. She was finally free to go her own way. The drive this time to Nana's was a good one. I was comfortable all the way. Daddy and I both talked openly about how Nana and Grandpa would take the fact that Mama had walked out on us.

Daddy was willing to stay with Mama for my sake but had told her that he could no longer trust her with me and I was all he had in the world and he would never let anything happen to me. He also had told mama that from now on, wherever he went, he was taking me with him. Mama didn't like the thought of me going with him leaving her at home alone, but daddy was sincere. It was as if Mama could not see that daddy loved her.

She wanted someone to rescue her the way she felt daddy was rescuing me from the things I was being exposed to. She was exposing me to situations that could have been dangerous and daddy knew it. He never thought mama would do such a thing, but she did. She could not take knowing that once again the man in her life spoke in the defense of his child and stood up for them but not her. Mama did not love herself enough. She always told me,

"You will see what men are like one day Naomi!"

"You'll see," she would say.

"I didn't understand anything she said Daddy, because I always thought you were a good dad."

"Thank you baby."

Daddy said. We rode quietly the rest of the way to Nana's house. Daddy put one hand on the steering wheel and reached and took hold of my hand and swallowed it up in his strong hands.

"It's going to be alright, pumpkin,

"I promise," Daddy said, as he set the car on cruise control. This part of the road to Nana's was very quiet. I leaned on his shoulder as best I could in my seat belt still holding onto his hand.

Now I finally felt safe. I never wanted to be anywhere else but here, sitting in the front seat of the car with daddy for the first time in my life. It seemed that one thing after another was changing in my life for the better. I only hoped the dreams would get better as well…only time would tell.

Author: Victoria E. Kain

~ CHAPTER 4 ~

Years of Lost Love

It seemed that when your life changes for the better under tragic situations, it takes time for everything to get back to normal. You ruminate over things that could have been done differently not knowing what you yourself could have done to change things, even if you could have done nothing at all. You always instinctively take some of the blame whether you were to blame or not. I guessed it was just being human. For some reason, the drive to Nana's seemed longer today. It could have been because of all the drama with Mama leaving daddy and me this weekend or me being traumatized by seeing these men in our home not knowing why they were there. Not that I am naive or anything but there are some things you just don't want to think about where your mother is concerned.

For that reason, I chose to stick with the thought that I didn't know why those men were there. It seemed that Daddy and I both were starting our lives all over again without Mama. For me it was like being born again as a baby, but this time with a parent that actually wanted me. While I knew I'd never forget her, it would be hard not to miss her being in my life. She will miss me graduating, going to college and even getting married someday, and maybe having children if I chose to. Even some of the cruel things Mama use to do to me I would laugh at them later after she did them because they made no since at all for a mother to do the things she did to her child.

Cease To Exist

I never told anyone, not even Nana about how Mama really treated me. I thought that silence and going into my mind where I was safe was the best way to deal with any pain I experienced. It seemed to be the only place where I could try to be myself. Many times mama would pull my hair and slap me for no reason and accuse me of looking like someone else other than who I was told was my daddy. It was as if the man she thought was my father, the one she really loved, didn't want her, and she would not want his child. She once burned me with her flat iron. She said it was an accident, but she was mad when daddy called and she had to get off the phone with one of her friends.

I believe she was haunted by the man she really wanted through me. I would cry during and after the abuse, but not for long, realizing that the verbal abuse would be over soon. She complained that I was too tanned, but she really wanted to be able to tan more herself so she put me down for something she couldn't naturally have. I now believe she was envious of my olive complexion. Daddy was tanned as well but Mama was very pale. So, I accepted the negative remarks and the beatings on my back and head. I knew the scars would heal on the outside, but prayed that the ones on the inside would heal as well. My mother hated the fact that my father was a handsome intelligent black man who adored me in every way. We never used the word "white" in our household as a way to respect Mama, so we used the term "pale," if we wanted to refer to the difference in our skin complexion.

Author: Victoria E. Kain

She was okay with that. Sometimes she would tell me that I looked like daddy, but she would shake her head in disdain as if it was a curse to look like him. Mama knew that daddy was handsome and I knew Mama was jealous of him. She always commented on how women would stare at him and smile all the time.

I stopped thinking about Mama for a moment and tried to get on with the acceptance that she was finally gone and free to live her life without destroying ours. I wondered if I would have as much fun as I normally did under better circumstances this summer as I sat waiting to arrive at Nana's. I had noticed that Ddaddy had become sad before we got to the stretch where we pulled up to Nana's front yard. I remembered when we passed the old Jacobs farm and looked across the land, that's when daddy began to cry. I couldn't believe all that had happened that day. But being there with Daddy was majestic for me. I was almost home. Daddy seemed to drive very slowly up through the gate and onto the front yard.

As we drove up on Nana and Grandpa Cody's yard, I could hardly wait to open the car door that seemed to weigh a hundred pounds. I could smell honey suckle in the air and pine needles from all the beautiful tall pine trees that bordered the farm. I could hardly wait to dash to my grandmother's arms and know a mother's love. I felt that God had not forgotten about me and gave me Nana to replace the affection I needed that he was aware that I did not get from Mama.

My heart was pounding as I finally let go of daddy's hand and almost opened the door while the vehicle was still in motion. My heart was about to burst with joy to see both of my Grandparents standing on the porch as if they were posing for a family portrait.

Although Grandpa Cody did not interact with us very much, he made his love known by the way he treated me whenever anyone was there. I still knew he loved me and was proud that I was his granddaughter. The time had finally come. My life was taking a turn for the better. The day had been so horrible that I had forgotten that it was my birthday. I realized I was 13 years old today and quickly accepted that this was why Nana bought me the dress. I was happy but sad about Mama and having to go through all of the things we had to go through. I wondered for a moment if the other kids on my block lost their parent the same way I did? Nana gave me a big hug like she had never seen me at all and it had only been a week since I had seen her and Grandpa. After hugging me, she looked up at daddy with a big smile and grabbed him,

"Come here, boy," Give me some sugar! She said to daddy.

"I am so glad to see you back safely!"

"You get more handsome each time you come back." She said.

Daddy was blushing as Nana hugged him and was grinning really hard.

"What you doing here so soon?"

"I thought you had six months left?" she asked. Finally Nana realized she didn't see Mama. She looked around for Mama like she really had lost something. She did not see her in the car. Then she looked back at daddy and her eyes dropped to the ground and she shook her head.

"She's gone isn't she?" Nana reluctantly asked reaching for her scarf on her head.

"Yes ma'am," daddy said, with a sad voice. Now looking off towards the lake as if he wanted to walk away and drown himself in it.

"You didn't hit her did you?" She quickly replied in a shaky voice like she was going to cry. Trying to validate whether she needed to be upset with daddy or not. You could tell she wanted to be mad at somebody other than Mama. She must have hated that they had argued the last time she saw her at the house.

"No ma'am, you know I gave you my word I would never hit her, but I can't say the same for the fella that was in my house with her." Nana, held her head down as if she was ashamed of Mama.

"Umph, umph, umph!"

"Lord have mercy!" she said.

"I knew my child was going to have man trouble all her life!"

"I just knew it!" Nana said, in a perplexed voice. It was understandable that she would feel this way because she only had one child and that was Mama. She loved her but they were never close and I never understood why.

"Where'd she go David?"

"I don't know Ms. Mattie," Peggy said she would let me know for Naomi's sake only.

"I really don't know."

"Well, did you finally tell her about Naomi?" She asked. Meaning, what daddy told me on the way to her house about me being his child through the paternity test.

"I did."

"She didn't take it well and that was why she felt relieved to finally be able to leave me."

"What happened son," Nana asked?

Daddy hesitated and began to tell the story of events that took place.

"Before she knew I was coming home, he said," I called her to tell her I was coming but she started an argument on the phone like she always did accusing me of being with another woman. I was at work and when I spoke to her again and I was in the airport when I called, some of the guys wives had come to pick them up and they were carrying on in the background. She yelled at me and told me that Naomi wasn't mine and that I should get someone to have a kid for me."

"I was so mad I just told her to shut up and I hung up the phone, knowing I would be there shortly and could talk to her and let her know everything would be alright.

"I was so embarrassed standing there with every other soldier being greeted by their wives with hugs and kisses and I called to tell mine I was coming home and I got to come home and see her with another man."

Daddy finally broke down and cried again. He wasn't ashamed to cry in front of them. I knew he was about to cry earlier but just needed another adult to cry on their shoulders because mine were too small. Nana hugged him and we walked up on the porch and sat down.

I looked and listened to all the conversation this time and no one asked me to leave the porch where they sat. I finally felt that they trusted me. Not like Mama always shooed me away when adults were talking. Nana and daddy felt I needed to know these things. Too much had happened for me to be kept in the dark anymore.

"Well, since you were always up front with me when Naomi was born I agreed to keep it a secret along with you." And I did." Nana said.

"Peggy needed to know what was in her heart. She could always draw a man in but she couldn't keep him long." Nana said. I didn't know what she meant about "drawing" a man Naomi thought. I guess some of the conversation I really didn't need to hear yet.

"Ms. Mattie, you know I loved Peggy," daddy said, almost in tears again.

"I knew that from the first moment I saw you with her," Nana jumped in to affirm his statement.

"But I also saw the faraway look in Peggy's eyes, like her heart was miles away."

"When she told me she was pregnant and didn't know who the baby's father was, I was scared for her, you and the baby but appreciated you being there with her."

"At first I thought you were not the father David and was a fool for staying, but then I saw the kind of man you really were." Nana said, her voice saddened.

"As I said, I fell in love with a woman that didn't love me." Daddy replied. "She gave me a beautiful daughter that loves me dearly! Isn't that right pumpkin?"

Now blushing, Naomi quietly leaned over and hugged her daddy.

"I do love you daddy!" I always will, no matter what.

They all sat quietly for a few moments and then Nana shook me gently.

"Go see what Grandpa got to show you," she said.

"I want to talk to your daddy some more just me and him."

"Okay, Nana!

I didn't feel so bad leaving the conversation because I had heard enough. I ran to the back by the corn field calling Grandpa. Daddy and Nana talked low for a long time. I stopped eavesdropping at that point.

Naomi was finally here with her loving Grandparents again... she always longed for this moment. Her grandmother's house seemed to be a safe haven for her. She felt that it allowed her to be where ever she wanted to be. She

Walked through the screened door to inspect the house that she had dreamed of all year. Walking very slowly, as if not to disturb someone that might be sleeping even though no one was there in the house but her. She looked around absorbing everything in sight. She longingly looked at the quaint old walls that she loved so much.

The old house only had five rooms but they were bigger than any rooms she had ever seen in such a small house. There was Nana and Grandpa's room that had a full size bed in it and a trunk at the foot with an old quilt that Nana's mother had made for her when she was first married. There were two other rooms for bedrooms and another room for sewing that Nana did as well. Then there was the kitchen which was across from Nana's room and one of the other bedrooms. There was a wood burning stove that had an oven and warmer above it. That was where all the leftover food was kept from the day's meals. The old wood box sat next to the stove and Grandpa Cody would keep it full of choice pieces of wood when Nana was cooking dinner or canning for the winter. I remembered every meal in that old kitchen and the love that was there while it was being prepared.

I remembered waking up each morning to birds singing outside my windows and sometimes they would land on the window ledge outside. The sun would be shining down on my face. Nana always said it was a pretty face…I never thought I was pretty but I believed her because it felt good. It was a little piece of heaven on earth for me to have these kinds of memories. Little did I know that these memories would soon make the difference between life and death for me? The whitewashed cabinet sat in a lonely corner of the kitchen behind the back door that led outside to the back porch. Everyone loved that cabinet because it held all of Nana's delicious baked goods.

Her peach cobblers and tea cakes were always fresh and tasty. Her eclectic array of old hand me down dishes graced her cupboards and her tables which indicated the simplicity of their lives, but it also showed the love they had for each other.

She never complained about her life with Grandpa Cody, although it was not a monetarily rich life, except for the love they had for each other. She canned fresh canned peaches and baked sweet potato pies and all sorts of goodies in that old kitchen that only had the basics. No chef's utensils or stainless steel counters you'd see in this old house. People came from miles away to get a taste of some of those cakes Nana made. It was truly the life I would always dream of.

Because there was no refrigerator in the house, anything that needed to be chilled, Nana would have Grandpa go into town, miles away and buy a block of ice and put it in a number three foot tub. He would get up early in the morning and would walk to get this ice. He usually took a small wagon with him to bring it back or he might catch a ride with someone that would bring him to the fork in the road and then he would walk down to the old farm house. They only did this when company was coming though on special occasions. Nana had a living room which most folks didn't have, but only company sat in there.

Cease To Exist

I was never allowed to play in that room and I understood. Occasionally I sat in there waiting for Nana on Sunday mornings before she got dressed for Sunday service. There was a radio on the table with a pink doily. There was a sofa and a chair and a coffee table. No one had that in these parts but Nana which indicated that in some ways, she was rich to many of the other folk that lived in that area who had much less than she did. The room next to that was Nana's sewing room which had a tiny elongated window with two dull white eyelet curtains that barely covered the surface of the window. It also faced the morning sun. She didn't have to use her glasses when she sewed in this room because she said that God's light fixed her eyesight when the sun was out.

In another room where I slept, there was a small bed in the corner that fit me perfectly. It was the prettiest room in the house. My three dolls and I occupied this space and we were the only ones that slept in this room. Two of my dolls had no hair but we slept comfortably in this room. Nana had given me these dolls when I was little and although I wanted to take them home each year, she would insist that I leave them out there and stated they would patiently wait for me to arrive every summer. She said that the dolls loved for me to take care of them and they patiently waited for me. It always gave me something to look forward to. I always would do just as I was doing now and examining everything to see if anything had changed since I was there last. I seemed to love the dolls that had no hair more than the ones that did.

For some reason, I felt closest to them as if they needed more than the other dolls did and it gave me a reason to belong to someone that needed me. Naomi kept those dolls dressed and always paraded them around the house, even though her Nana was appalled by the sight of them now because they were tattered and torn. This old house was a beautiful home to Naomi, it meant everything to her. She was glad to be there this summer and could not wait to see her friends in the country. As she stepped to the back door and out on the back porch, she finally found Grandpa Cody coming from the old worn down barn.

"Hey there lil bit," he blurted out! He had called me that since I was knee high to everything.

"You all growed up tall since I saw you on Saturday!" He said, not caring that his grammar was horrible...I didn't much care either. When you are in the country, you speak the way you want to and you don't have to pretend. Grandpa Cody made the only joke he knew how, and smiled showing all his tobacco stained teeth or at least the ones he had left.

"Hey papa Cody, Naomi called him playfully. It was the name only she called him sometimes.

"I missed you and Nana, and I couldn't wait to get here." Naomi gave papa Cody a big hug.

"Where's your Mama?" Papa asked. Naomi was quiet for a moment. She wasn't sure how to answer. He could see the look in her eye and asked her again. "Naomi, did you hear me gal, I asked you a question, where's your Mama?" He said in a kind but authoritative voice, "Daddy's home papa."

Quietly, putting her head down, the tried to busy herself with the ants on the ground by her feet.

"You wait right here for me baby," Papa said, with a bit of anxiousness in his voice. He didn't want me to know how concerned he was but since he didn't know anything about what had happened, he was very nervous and concerned that I had not answered his question to his satisfaction.

"Let me go say hey to your daddy"! He said, trying to make light of what I had just told him. He knew something was wrong and I could see that look in his eyes. He patted his back pocket like he always did before he went outside to check on things at night if the dogs barked and he heard something.

I also knew that Papa Cody kept his pistol with him as well. I always heard Nana telling him, 'Cody don't go out there shooting yourself in the foot like no fool now!' you hear me! Nana would say. I didn't think he was going to shoot daddy or anything but I didn't know what was about to go down.

"I'll be right back." Papa mumbled. He hadn't even got to the end of the house before he ushered out another order.

"You stay right here now, don't go poking around and get bit by no snake!"

"I aint sucking no poison outta nobody today!"

"I won't papa!" Naomi said, smiling as if he had just complimented her. She knew that if she got bit by anything papa would lose his life trying to save hers.

She was so confident that she was loved and that nothing could harm her on this piece of land with Nana and papa that even with her Mama leaving it didn't hurt as bad when she got here to the old farm. She knew she would be all right. Naomi hurried and stationed herself on the back porch steps and busied herself looking at the trail of ants that led to a dead bug feast. She wondered what happened to the bug and hated to see anything harmed so she focused her attention on something else. Nana and I had planted two peach trees two summers ago and now the peaches were huge on those trees. I couldn't wait to eat one but dared take one without permission. There were so many that she couldn't count them all.

"One, two, three, four...as she counted the prettiest ones first, then there was a short silence as she wondered what the adults were talking about and hoped daddy was okay. Before she could think further, she heard voices finishing her count down of the peaches..."Five, six, seven, a voice finished counting that she didn't recognize." Before eight could come out, Naomi looked over and there they were, her two best friends, Patrice and Shellie walking into the back yard!

"Oh, my goodness!"

"You're here!!!!!" Naomi screamed, running to the girls and literally jumping on them both with a bear hug. They hugged each other and carried on some much commotion that papa and daddy came to see what was going on with all the yelling and screaming. Grandpa Cody even had his gun drawn thinking something had happened until Naomi spoke.

"Daddy, its Patrice and Shellie!!!" Do you remember them Daddy?" she yelled.

"I do." Daddy said, smiling approvingly, knowing my summer would be okay even with all that had happened. He looked at Nana who had entered the back porch through the house and was looking on through the screen door as she smiled a sad smile. You could tell she felt bad that mama had left us. She knew that we would be okay regardless. I was truly happy and would take the time to sit and talk with my friends as Grandpa Cody came back to the chicken area and spoke to me and my friends.

"Who all want to go see the baby pigs?"

"We do papa Cody!" They all said in unison.

"Then come on!" he said, as he led the way down to the hog pen. Not that it was a pretty sight for us. It was just that it was something else to do to take our minds off mama leaving us. I looked back as daddy smiled watching me walk away. I turned around to go back and give him a big hug, which he eagerly accepted.

"I love you so much daddy!"

"I love you too pumpkin." He said.

"You go on and have some fun with your friends." "I'm going to stay for dinner with you all and then head home. I am really tired." Naomi was so happy her daddy was staying for supper. Her grandpa finally beaconed for her and her friends to come down to where he was. He asked if they were ready to see the piglets and they all said yes, realizing that they were getting older and weren't as excited as they use to be when they were younger.

But they humored Grandpa Cody anyway. They saw the little piglets and whispered that someday they would become bacon and ham on someone's breakfast plate. Naomi and her friends laughed so hard at the thought of it although they really didn't want the piglets to be hurt but knew they were being groomed for that fateful day. "Wow, how would it feel if you knew you were being fed only to feed someone else on another day?"

I couldn't even think about that and decided not to think about the fate of the poor little pigs. I wanted to get reacquainted with Shellie and Patrice again. We all walked back up to the house and sat on the porch and talked until the sun was going down. We played with each other's hair and measured to see who's was the longest. Mine was the longest and then there was Patrice and Shellie. We checked to see who had budded more and exchanged information about our training bra sizes and neither one of us had much to brag about in this area but we all had the dreaded cycle that our moms use to talk about.

This went on for a couple of hours until Nana turned on the kitchen light and started supper. Shellie and Patrice both had to go home and daddy and I walked then down the road while Nana cooked. It was a bad day because of Mama, but a beautiful day because I finally felt like I was free and not in prison... I could only imagine what it would feel like to be in prison and not know why you were there.

Rotting away with no one to love you. It would be a cruel way for someone to live their life. I wanted the rest of my vacation and my life to feel this good but for some reason, I knew I would have to work hard to keep it this way. I prayed that it would. Daddy and I walked back from Patrice and Shellie's house. It was getting dark but daddy walked tall and confident. I took the precious time to talk to my daddy alone with on one to shoo me away. It felt wonderful. "Daddy, are you scared to be out at night like this?" I asked. He reached for my hand and held it.

"No baby,"

"I've been in some really dangerous situations where people wanted to harm me and I might have to protect myself, so this is nothing."

'He wasn't scared at all,' I whispered to myself. I felt safe just knowing that daddy wasn't afraid. I wondered what Mama was doing right now, but quickly threw the thought out of my head as a chill came over me. The day would be good. Nana fixed a good dinner and Grandpa said the grace. We ate together as a family for the first time. It was as if mama was not even missed, but I know we all did miss her. Daddy ate dinner and then finally got ready to go back to the city. Sleep would be good for me tonight.

I wouldn't have to look at the American flag and see the ugly covers on my bed, or sleep in a house with strange men in it. Not knowing if one would eventually try to attack me. I wished Patrice and Shellie had stayed for dinner with us.

We all sat around the old table and talked for a long while. It was as if we wanted to insure that we all were working through mama being gone from our lives. As they talked grown folk talk, I recanted in my head what we had just had for dinner. It was always good food at Nana's. Tonight she had whipped up the best meal ever. She cooked fried chicken, mashed potatoes and gravy and hot biscuits with broccoli casserole, my favorite.

Her sweet tea was ever better. Daddy enjoyed himself and sat next to me. He held my hand for a brief moment under the table every time I believe he thought about mama. I could see the sad look in his eye and wished I could fix his sadness but knew no one could. Nana cleaned the dishes and even though I tried to help, she shooed us all out of her kitchen because we took too long. We laughed and had the most fun ever…it was as if we had become like a new family. Over the years, Shellie and Patrice had become like the sisters I never had but always wanted. Before they had left that night, we vowed that we would always be there for each other. No matter what the need or where we were.

We would seek out and find each other. No more fear for now. Daddy finally left to go back to the city. I hated for him to be alone, but he insisted. Nana talked to him before he left and he was alright. He knew we loved him and I said goodbye.

Author: Victoria E. Kain

Me and Nana sat in the swing after dinner on the porch while Grandpa Cody lay on the end of the porch like a guard dog and napped as he always did before making his last security check around the house for the night before going in to bed. Nana sang a sad song tonight, denoting her inner feelings for the loss of her only daughter who was finally free. As I leaned on her soft shoulder, I felt love like I had never felt it before.

This would be the one emotion that I would learn to nurture for the rest of my natural life. We sat in the swing on the front porch for a long time and watched the moon which was lit up in the sky. We could see the red tail lights from daddy's car going onto the highway from Nana and Grandpa's house. I watched the lights until I could no longer see them at all. It was as part of me had just left. For the first time in my life, I wanted to go back home because I knew I had someone there that actually wanted me there. Now I was sure of it and nothing could change it for me…I was going to be okay.

~ CHAPTER 5 ~

Turning Back Time

Naomi awakened in the morning to the beautiful sunlight beaming through the tiny bedroom window. She had dreamed of this day and felt like a princess in her own private castle. The new clean white eyelet curtains Nana had bought from town the year before hung neatly over the wood framed window in her room. When Naomi was a little girl, Nana always said that those curtains would never block God's beautiful sun from warming her pretty face each morning. To this day, the sun still would light up her room and warm her heart as she lay in bed.

Even at a grand old age of 13 years now, she still gave attention to her dolls who had been her faithful companions throughout childhood. Naomi was loyal even to them and would not discard them ever regardless of their physical wear and tear. They had been there from the beginning with her, so she felt she owed them that. They were like her family when her daddy was gone. She pretended to be their mother but treated them well. Not like her Mama treated her and never talked to her about anything. Today, in the aftermath of her mother leaving them, she lay in bed waiting for Nana to call her in for breakfast. Even though many times she was already awake when Nana called, she would just lay there playing with my dolls until she heard the sound of her sweet voice.

Author: Victoria E. Kain

She anticipated when she would call by the smell of the bacon frying and biscuits in the oven with hot grits. Lying in bed fiddling with the covers and the matching pillow case fringes is what she did. Looking around the room as if she were a princess waiting for servants to come in and dress her for the day. Her eyes searched the room with anticipation. Finally, the voice she waited to hear calls out...

"Naomeee," she yells, in a sweet authoritative voice.

"Time to eat breakfast, baby!" she would say. I had waited all year to get here for the summer to hear my name being called in a sweet way. It was truly music to my ears. Naomi, quickly slid out of bed and jumped in the clothes that were neatly laid out on the foot of her bed by her grandmother the night before as if little elves had been working all night to make sure everything matched. There was the pretty pink shirt and matching shorts with white sandals that she had packed along with ribbons for her ponytail. They were all perfectly laid out. Even though she was 13 now, she was still innocent and didn't mind the pampering of an eight year old. Most teenagers would baulk at this type of attention, but not Naomi.

She loved being cared for the way parents should care for their children. All the while Naomi dressed, she was grinning like a Cheshire cat. Before she even left her bedroom, she was drooling from the sweet smell of the bacon and biscuits her grandmother had made from scratch.

"Ummm," Naomi thought,

"I can't wait to get to the table for a real meal!"

She rushed into the little kitchen almost toppling over the crate that held the wash pan where everyone washed their face and hands. It was interesting that you brushed your teeth out on the back porch and spit out the water on the ground. I guess it made sense not to use the same pan you wash your face in. Besides, Nana knew how to keep us clean and safe. There was always a bar of homemade potash soap on the side of the wash basin on an old saucer Nana had been given by a neighbor years ago. The soap always smelled fresh and I know it was because Nana made it from the fat that was rendered from the animal they killed for food. They never threw away anything but used it all. I remember one year seeing her make it in that same black pot she used to boil water for bleaching clothes and other things. She would make enough to last for a while and to give other people some.

I finally took the piece of soap and lathered my hands first. Nana always taught me to do that so I could control the amount of soap that was on my face. The soap smelled nice with a clean fresh sent to it and it is soft and sometimes hard to gauge how much soap you are actually using. Naomi soon realizes that she had too much soap on her face and tries to wash it off but there doesn't seem to be enough water in the basin to take it off fast enough. Her eyes are tightly shut and she is now in complete darkness. She begins to panic, but remembers that there are always two towels hanging on a nail beside the door.

As she reached for the towel with her face still wet and her eyes tightly closed, she cannot find those towels. She keeps reaching frantically but does not want to open her eyes for fear she will get soap in them. Naomi really begins to panic now, because she cannot find those towels that are always there on the wall. She also hated being in the dark and even though she knows that Nana is in the kitchen with her, she did not want her to know that she had done exactly what she was told not to do by lathering too much soap. Just when she was about to give in and confess by asking for help, she slightly feels the soft cotton of one of the towels on her hand. Her grandmother had quietly observed her distress and reached over and shifted the towel towards her flailing hands to halt her misery, but did not say a word. It was as if to allow Naomi the feeling of accomplishment by finding it on her own.

Naomi quickly dried off her face and hands and Nana walks over and took the dipper out of the water bucket and poured more water in the basin for her to rinse her face again. She knew she still had soap on it and didn't want her skin to become irritated. When her face was finally cleaned off, she looked at her grandmother and gave her a big smile and an even bigger hug.

"I love you Nana." Naomi said.

"Yeah, I know you do sugar," her grandmother said.

"You love me because I made these biscuits you like so much," she said. She knew well that was the reason she made the special breakfast for her darling Naomi.

Cease To Exist

"Nana, I love you because I love you!" Naomi said. She then made me a small plate for breakfast. I smiled and sat down to eat because I was very hungry and relieved that I did not have to stay in the darkness any longer. It made her remember her bad dream she had had that night. Naomi hated the dark and had been having more bad dreams at home before she came to Nana's. She wasn't sure if it was because of how her Mama treated her or now because she had left them altogether. She wanted to tell Nana about the dreams. She now could openly talk to her about it without worrying if she would tell her Mama.

She begins telling her grandmother about the strange dreams she had been having for a while and as she rambles on and on, her grandmother listens intently as Naomi unfolds the recurring dreams. She also told her how her mama would lock her in her room since she was a very little girl and she could come out sometimes for the whole weekend. Her Nana, seemed sad all over again so she only talked about the dreams and not her Mama. She didn't want to hurt her Nana, knowing that she still loved her mama. "Every night it seems that I am dreaming that I can't find my light switch in the bedroom to turn on the light. I get frightened Nana, as if I am confined somewhere."

"When I get frightened in the dark, Naomi said, I find myself reaching frantically for the light switch. I desperately want to turn the light on so I can see!" Her grandmother looks over her eyeglasses with a furred brow, as if to inspect Naomi to see if she is telling the truth.

Author: Victoria E. Kain

"You mean, like you were searching for the towel this morning?" her grandmother asked.

"Yes, just like that." Naomi said, surprised that her grandmother saw that towel and was the one who halted the panic episode she would have experienced if she hadn't put the towel within reach. Nana had not mentioned it until now. Naomi went on to say...

"And it seems as if there is a stale odor in the room too when I have this dream." Her grandmother looked at Naomi with a frown again. This time, she wondered if there was a snake around the house outside somewhere. The old saying was that rattle snakes have an old musty smell. She reminded herself that she needed to do a general cleaning on that room, since no one goes in there until Naomi comes out in the summer. She had told papa Cody to put down some sulfur to ward off snakes. Nana also thought it could be dirty socks under Naomi's bed as well from the musty smell she encountered. She also wondered if Naomi was sad about her mother leaving and had begun having nightmares. She went back to the fact that Naomi would sometimes leave her dirty laundry in a pile under the corner of her bed. She had good intent to get them in the wash but would forget and be afraid to tell Nana.

'She really does not keep that room tidy,' her grandmother thought. "What else happened in your dream?" Her grandmother recanted, as if trying to appease Naomi while she ate her breakfast.

"Nana, there was also a loud noise and a clanking sound like metal doors closing."

"I thought it was you or granddaddy closing the back door to the barn."

"I know how you have to pull it up real hard to make it close right."

"Anyway, the dream scares me every time I dream it." Naomi said.

"Well just don't think about it too much honey and stop eating candy before you go to bed!" Her grandmother gently scolded.

Nana didn't want to make me feel bad by bringing up the fact that Mama was gone now. She used every excuse she could find to ensure that I didn't have nightmares.

"I want to hear more about your dreaming," Nana repeated, as if I didn't hear her the first time.

"Right now, we need to get this buttermilk down to Miss Amy.

"She's not feeling so good these days since she lives by herself now."

"You can go with me and talk to me on the way if you'd like."

"Yes Ma'am." I'll get dressed. Naomi put the dream on hold for a while. She is excited that the day will be filled with things to do with her grandma. They always took milk to old lady Amy's house. I don't know why that's all Nana ever gave Ms. Amy to eat, unless she is a cat, she needs more to eat than milk, Naomi thought.

We never stayed there long because Nana said Ms. Amy's house smelled like old rubber. I don't know what that meant except that she did not like the smell and would go in and take her the milk and say her quick greetings and then leave real fast. I watched Nana quickly wrap her hair up in a head rag carefully ensuring that all of her brown curly hair was covered under the rag. I wondered why she always did that and decided to ask.

"Nana, why do you wrap your hair up when you walk down the road?" I asked.

"Well, baby, I don't want all the dust and dirt to get in my hair if a car goes by. I would have to wash my hair every night if I didn't wrap it up.

That was a good answer she gave, but it didn't completely satisfy me. My hair was even longer than Nana's, so why don't I have a head scarf too? I quietly waited for a moment and then popped the next question.

"Nana, my hair is awful heavy, shouldn't I have a head rag too?" Hoping she'd say yes and I could look just like her.

"Well, she said, you do have long thick hair and lord knows I don't want to fool with that head of hair tonight."

"Besides, I just changed those sheets on your bed too.

"Yes, take this old head rag and wrap up your hair." She said. I hurried and wrapped up my hair and she helped me so that none was left out. I was grinning really hard and she lightly pinched my cheeks and smiled.

"Let's hurry and take this milk to Ms. Amy."

"Yes Nana, I answered.

We hurried down the steps and out to the road to Ms. Amy's. Nana yelled to Grandpa Cody,

"I'll be back in a minute," she said. She didn't get a response from Grandpa, but knew he heard her wherever he was, even if he was down at the hog pen. We began walking down the road and I held Nana's hand for a moment pretending it was Mama. Finally we got to Ms. Amy's yard. It was all grown up with weeds. Nana grabbed my hand and pulled me behind her.

"Don't go any further than where you see me going, you hear!"

"Yes, Ma'am," I said. We walked up to the porch and Nana called out to Ms. Amy.

"Ms. Ameeeee!" She said, in a squeal like voice as if she was calling hogs.

"It's me and Naomi coming to bring your milk!" We didn't hear anything and finally a faint voice came out from the depths of the old shack.

"Come on up, Mattie!" She replied.

We walked up the rickety steps and Nana whispered to me, "Don't come in the house with me, the floor boards are rotten and it might be too heavy for both of us." I nodded accepting her counsel to stay put on the porch. Ms. Amy came closer to the door and invited Nana and me in, but first asked, "Who is this young lady?"

"This is my granddaughter, Naomi."

"You remember her don't you?" Nana asked,"

"Mind your manners Naomi." Nana said. Making sure I spoke to Ms. Amy.

"Hello Ms. Amy." I said,

"You are all grown up child," she said.

"Would y'all like to come in and have some milk with me?" She asked.

Nana quickly stated,

"No, we got supper to make so we'll be getting back."

"Cody is cutting wood for the stove now. Thank you anyway!"

"Let me take the milk bucket in for you." Ms. Amy opened the door that almost came apart in her hand. Nana reluctantly walked in and moved about as if she were in a mine field trying not to step on a mine and be blown to bits. She finally made it to the kitchen table and back to the front porch and rolled her eyes up to the sky mouthing the words, "Thank God I made it." I did everything to keep from laughing...Nana was funny when she wanted to be.

We prepared to leave and walked slowly down the steps taking every precaution not to fall through the wooden steps. When we made it to the bottom of the steps, Nana would say in a light shrilly voice,

"Ms. Amy, you take care yourself, you hear!" as she hurriedly walked down the steps holding onto the rickety rails that were falling apart. Ms. Amy did not have anyone living at the house with her. Her kids were all grown and lived up north and her husband had died a few years earlier.

In short, everything in the house was falling apart, to include Ms. Amy. As we walked away from the house, I looked back to watch Ms. Amy slowing turn around to walk back into her little house. The dark opening looked as if it just swallowed her frail body up as she finally disappeared into the black hole of a house. As we walked along the dirt road, I picked up rocks that looked interesting and threw them across the field. It kept me occupied as Nana sang some religious hems under her breath, never seeming to know all the words, but would just hum the melody anyway. Nana would stop singing and warned me not to get too close to the bushes because a snake could be lying in the grass. I hated snakes. I paid attention to what she said because I really hated snakes and didn't want to get bitten by one.

She always said that, Ms. Amy's husband was bitten by a rattle snake and never got better until he died. As we turned the bend to go into the stretch for the old house, we saw Ms. May Louise Taylor sitting on her porch rocking. All the women on this road were elderly or widows. She was the nosey neighbor who always spied on everyone whenever they went somewhere. People in the country liked her because she was better than having a guard dog they said. Ms. Taylor would always let you know if she saw or heard anything near your place. Sometimes she would see things and folks that weren't even there. Besides, she always had a story to tell so some of the things she saw she just made them up. We figured that was because she was so old. She had to be at least 90. I don't know why they even took her word for anything at that age, but they did.

As Naomi and her grandmother walked along the old road, Naomi was skipping about and circling her grandmother because she was so slow; she looked over and saw what appeared to be a lizard lying on the side of the road, dead. Being a very sensitive child Naomi hated to see anything hurt or wounded. She asked her grandmother what it was, and her grandmother stopped for a moment and adjusted her glasses downward so she could get a closer look at the lizard. Finally she said,

"That's an old chameleon."

Naomi immediately asked

"What happened to it? Why does it look like that," she asked, looking at the dead critter in the middle of changing his colors.

He looked as if he was a cross between the dirt on the road and the bushes alongside the road. Her grandmother just looked at her and said,

"Baby, that old chameleon, didn't change fast enough.

"Naomi repeated her grandmother's words in her head, "he didn't change fast enough? She said. She didn't quite understand what Nana meant but she didn't dare ask her again which would show that she wasn't paying attention. Her grandmother hated it when she had to repeat herself and would have scolded Naomi. Naomi knew she would have to find out what her Nana meant by the statement she made about the chameleon. Naomi waited until they arrived home and she hurried to her room and grabbed the old dictionary off the dusty shelf.

She looked up chameleon and began to eagerly read the meaning of the word silently at first, as if to ensure that she had digested it. Then she boldly repeated the words aloud, as if she had an audience listening because she understood what her grandmother meant when she said, "he didn't change fast enough."

The chameleon has to adapt to his new surroundings immediately in order to survive. He could not afford to hesitate. She repeated the words. His instinct tells him that he must act quickly in order not to become something else's prey. Naomi paused for a moment and looked away from the book. As she stared out of her bedroom window thinking about what she had read, it began to get dark. She realized that people were like chameleons too. They must adapt quickly to various situations in life or they could be lost forever.

Even though Naomi was very young still, her life was dictating that she learn things very quickly. Childhood for her seemed to be fleeting with every dream she had which caused her to look at things, people and life differently. She now understood that even with her mama, she had to make the change she made in her life in order to survive, whatever way she could.

People have to change throughout life with various situations that exist. If they don't quickly adapt during trials, they would not be able to cope with the ongoing mini traumas they must deal with. Naomi began to understand more about how the chameleon's life mimicked hers.

Author: Victoria E. Kain

She reasoned that living with her mama presented many challenges and she had to change daily to survive because her daddy was not there to protect her. She recalled how she instinctively locked her door and barricaded it at a young age, not knowing all the details of why she did it, but instinct told her it was the right thing to do. She wanted to stop daydreaming and began enjoying the rest of her summer at Nana's house because her life seemed to be fleeting away from her.

After all, Shellie and Patrice were here and they were her true friends. She knew they would have fun this summer. She wanted to spend the rest of her summer enjoying the sunshine and playing outside, picking blackberries that grew along the old fence line on the back road to the lake. She would always remember these days and made a conscious decision not to think any more about the mundane things for adults. She would be a child for now remembering that her mother never had the chance to be one...Life was good for Nomi...But it would soon be short lived.

~ CHAPTER 6 ~

A Lesson Learned

The next two summers were just as fun as all the rest before Mama left daddy and me. Daddy was never quite the same after Mama left but he seemed to be doing much better than when it first happened. I know it had to hurt him to be jilted like that. Either way, he became overly protective of me when I hit 15 years of age. He wanted to know where I was going, who I was going with, and where they lived. Crazy things like that. Things that I didn't think made much sense for him to know. But he wanted to know anyway. Since I was old enough to take care of myself I figured I could have at least one guy friend that was safe. Frankie was the school nerd but he was nice. When I wanted to go to the Mall or a ball game for school, he was my buddy. Daddy didn't mind me talking to him but one day he got it in his head to ask Frankie if he had been circumcised!!!

Frankie was mortified! He almost choked on his soda! "Really daddy!" I said, looking at him like he had two heads. "Why would you need to know that when I am not even sexually active?" "Frankie is still a virgin as well!" Naomi screamed! The teenage years had begun taking over and Naomi was in full bloom. Frankie just politely got up and left without saying goodbye. Naomi was incensed that her father would embarrass her and the boy like that.

Author: Victoria E. Kain

"I am not into that yet Daddy and besides, can you imagine how you have traumatized someone else's child!!!" She exclaimed, flicking her hair and rolling her eyes like a typical teenager. Daddy only shrugged his shoulders as if he had just asked someone to pass the ketchup at the dinner table or something and asked me if I wanted to ride with him to the Hardware store. It was literally nothing to him. I politely told him he could go alone and to remember that there are "Males" in the hardware store, trying to be sarcastic.

He quietly thought for a moment and stated, "Oh, you are right! You stay here till I get back." He walked out of the door. At that point I was mortally wounded with embarrassment. I never spoke to Frankie again after that. He actually was the only one that would go to the mall with me and not try anything stupid and now daddy had messed that up. Needless to say it was awkward seeing him at school after that.

He would literally see me I school and almost kill himself trying not to make eye contact with me and put his back pack in front of his groin as if I had ex-ray vision and was looking to see if he was actually circumcised or not. He probably wasn't. I had to simply let it go. It was too much to deal with along with occasional acne. This was another horrible page in my teenage diary to write. These years were awkward for me but I finally realized they were probably the same for daddy since he was raising me by himself and I was a girl instead of a boy. Hopefully we would survive.

Daddy had a lot on his mind these days. Weeks after the embarrassment of my only friend, he received orders to go to Germany. We had to sit down and talk about whether I would go with him or stay with Nana. I didn't want to leave Nana and Grandpa, but I didn't want Daddy to leave me here either and wasn't sure if I wanted to go to Germany. Mama had never wanted to go with daddy and I never understood why. I always wanted to go wherever he went, but Mama always made excuses to say no. We missed out on a lot of nice places to go. Daddy had been to Paris, Venice, Switzerland, Panama and so many nice places. Now I would not have to hear that I couldn't go. It was finally my choice.

"Well Naomi," daddy said, Are you going with me or not?" Those words rang in my ears and I loved the sound of it. My daddy wanted me to go with him. After all my young years, I was finally clear that I was his family. I belonged. Even my half-brothers never contacted us after mama left. It was strange, but I didn't care.

"Yes daddy, I want to go to Germany!"

"Great!" He said, jumping out of the chair, picking me up like I was a rag doll and twirling me around like I was as light as a feather.

"This will be fun!" I said. Daddy had expected that I would decline his offer, but I fooled him. I guess he had been so use to being told "no" in the past.

Author: Victoria E. Kain

"We will have a ball!" I will let the Colonel know tomorrow that they can process my orders. We will have a few months before I actually leave so this will be wonderful. I will take you to all of the places I have been and introduce you to some of my friends I made when I was there. Some of them have kids your age as well…this will be so great! He said. Daddy was really happy!

"You sure you want to go now?" Daddy asked, making sure he was not being happy for nothing.

"Don't get over there and start talking about you want to come home because home is where we both are, once we say yes!"

"No daddy," I am sure.

"What about your trio pack?" He asked, as if to make sure no issues would arise.

"You, Patrice and Shellie? Is leaving them going to cripple you?"

"Nope!" I fired back. It will be great.

"Okay, then, let's do this!" He said, walking out in the back yard. Daddy was in a great mood, so this was my chance to ask daddy if I could have a summer job before we left. I know he didn't want me to, but I figured that I did not want to work over there. This was a good time to ask and I hoped he would let me. I walked out on the patio and daddy was fidgeting with the grill to make it ready for steaks for dinner.

"Daddy, since we are going overseas, I wanted to know if I could earn some money before we get ready to go."

"Well, you can wash my truck for me," daddy said with a side grin…Mama never liked that grin, but it tickled me.

He reminded me of the villain on the movie I watched once where the guy would wax his mustache, before he attacked someone.

"No daddy, I mean a real job." Naomi said

"You mean like working for someone else?"

"Yes sir!" I could earn enough money to keep you from having to give me allowances at least for a few months.

"Where would you work Naomi?" Daddy asked, raising his brow way higher than I thought he ever could. I knew that meant he didn't agree.

"You know I don't like you being out at night Naomi."

"It will be a day job daddy," Naomi said, looking off in the distance making little eye contact with him so she wouldn't spook him. She took a deep breath and blurted it all out and then held her breath for the bomb to drop.

"Working at the barber shop as a manicurist."

"You always said I do my nails very nicely…. Now I can work on my craft." Naomi was still nervous, holding her nails up to the sunlight that was coming in through the living room window to bolster her case.

"BARBERSHOP!" he daddy yelled. You would have thought she had said she wanted to work in a strip club.

"You mean, where guys go and talk about everything under the sun???" He lamented, now huffing in a gruff voice, while shaking his head in disagreement.

"No daddy, not like that!" Naomi said, trying to convince her daddy it was okay because most of the teenaged girls worked summer jobs babysitting and besides her classmate's father owned the shop and let her work there to earn money. It was mostly cleaning up the barber shop. She continued pleading her case for the summer job.

"Well, one of my classmates father owns the barbershop, and… he is a minister as well." She said, holding her breath, thinking that piece of information would nail the deal. She still waited for the hammer to fall. She knew her daddy owed her something for running her only guy friend away from her.

"Where is this shop Naomi?"

"It's on Oak view street daddy, in the shopping plaza right behind the little theater in town. You remember don't you?"

"I know where that is." He grumbled,

"Well, I will have to think about this, Naomi, I don't have a good feeling about this."

"And furthermore, if I agree, and that is a giant if," I will have to do a sneak run there and have a shave and a haircut to see what the atmosphere is like." "They won't know me from Adam and I can see for myself. That way I will have my answer."

"Fair enough?" He asked, giving her the answer she wanted which was a "maybe" and not a flat "no."

"Dang it," Naomi thought! This will be no fun at all if daddy goes snooping too deep and let on that he is my dad. What if there are cute boys in there? She pondered. 'Well, I may not even get the job.' He is bound to find something wrong. Either way, I knew he was trying to protect me, I guess.

I knew how daddy was thinking. These are men in the shop and I am a girl and his little girl at that. "But I am 15!!! Mama treated me like a baby and I went nowhere and now daddy watches me like a hawk...

'Lighten up!' she thought. Naomi felt her daddy was sometimes too protective. She slowly walked out of the room and they had no further conversation about the matter.

It was just a timing issue now for him to check things out. Sure enough, her daddy did what he said he'd do. The next week, he went to the barber shop and got a shave and a haircut. When he returned, to Naomi's surprise he did not have anything bad to say about it. He was actually pleased that the conversations were very upbeat and respectful. The location was well lit and it was a busy day so he could get a good feel of what the atmosphere was like. Her Daddy even commented on the fact that the owner's daughter seemed to have everyone's respect. So he said "yes".

"Thank you daddy!!!" Naomi said.

"I will make sure that I do my chores here at home as well, I promise. Her dad gave her a hug and a warning to be careful. She couldn't wait to go to school and tell Beverly, her school mate that she had permission to apply for the job. She could only work three or four hours a day and on Friday and Saturday because she wasn't 16 yet but that was okay. It gave Naomi some experience.

Her classmate Beverly was strange sometimes at school and she acted much older than she was. Sometimes she even appeared a bit promiscuous. That was odd since her dad was a minister but I knew that I was still innocent and I thought she was too but would soon find out that was being naive on my part.

I filled out the application and gave it to her and to my surprise her father called me the next day for the interview. Daddy thought that was awfully fast, but since she was a school mate he figured that it was because she knew me and recommended me to her father. Either way, I went for the interview or he was very nice. He was a bit overweight, but I could overlook that as long as he paid me for my work. I answered all of his questions and he told me that I had the job. I started the job and it seemed okay at first. Each day, my school mate would come into the shop and her dad would give her this big kiss and hug.

I thought they were very affectionate but didn't think much about it. Daddy often hugged me, but not like my school mate's father hugged her when no one was looking.

It looked strange. Come to think of it, all of the people in the shop looked at her strange I wondered why daddy didn't notice that. Maybe he did and just thought nothing of it. I decided to ignore it as well which was a big mistake. The men that came in looked at me in a different way.

If I didn't have customers, I would sweep the area and tidy up the bathrooms. I got my first paycheck and had not manicured anyone the first week. Finally one week, I had my first manicure. I also received a very large tip. Ten dollars! I felt so good and thought this would be a great job. Daddy would normally pick me up from the barbershop but he had to go to the field the next week and he tried to get one of his friends to pick me up. I told daddy that my schoolmate and her dad would bring me home.

He was coming in late that night so I didn't need Miss Annie to come over and stay with me. Daddy didn't like the idea of the man bringing me home alone but I assured him that his daughter was always with us. So he agreed.

This night the preacher would be taking me home after he closed his shop and that was fine. I would get home when the sky was just getting dark.

It was always right before dusk. Every other time his daughter would come to the shop before he closed and would ride with us. This night he came over in a strange way and looked at me funny...

"Beverly is at her friend's house and we will stop by and pick her up on the way home. I will take you home after that." Okay.

"Yes sir, I said,"

"Daddy went to the field earlier and will get in later tonight." I said, without thinking.

"Oooh, your daddy's not home?" He asked.

The way he said it made me nervous and I thought about the villain and the slick mustache right before he did something mean. I quickly recanted,

"Oh he will be home soon!"

"Probably not long after I get in or he might already be there." I said, trying to make it sound like I would not be alone. My heart was racing a bit now but I didn't let on. I didn't like the idea that Beverly was not with us.

"You can sit up front if you'd like." He said,

I jumped at the chance since Mama never let me sit up front and had no reason to see anything wrong with it. Besides, I was older now.

We always had basic conversation. But this evening, the minister was talking to me about whether I had a boyfriend or not. I told him I wasn't allowed to date boys and he laughed.

"You mean you are not dating anyone?"

"No sir", I said, feeling a bit awkward talking about boys with this grown man, since I was not interested in them yet. I then asked him, "How long will it be before we get to where Beverly is?" It was taking a long time to get to her.

"Oh relax, we are almost there." He said.

"Actually, I need to stop by my friend's house and pick up some more clippers for tomorrow." We have a new barber coming in and I have an ad running in the paper to bring in new customers. I am building the business."

Naomi was getting nervous now, wondering what was going on. She was smart enough to know when someone was trying to trick her. Then she heard the words that she will never forget. It was something about these words that spooked her. "Trust me Naomi, and don't tell my daughter I took you here because she likes this guy's son and will be mad at me if she knew you came with me, being such a pretty girl as you are."

"How about it will be our secret." The preacher said. That is when Naomi knew that this was a lie. She remembered her mother's boyfriends winking at her in the kitchen and telling her, that everything was to be a "Secret!" She finally realized what was about to happen and yelled "NO!!!"

"I said, "No" Mr. Latimer!"

"If you could just drop me off first I would appreciate it because my daddy will be worried."

I tried to be polite because after all he was my ride home and it was customary to be polite. I wanted to believe I could trust him; after all, he was a minister! When I asked him to take me home first, he seemed nervous. He began to sweat even with the air conditioner on full blast in the vehicle to the point you could have frozen meat in there. I felt that because he was overweight and nervous, this was nervous perspiration.

Author: Victoria E. Kain

Cease To Exist

Even though I asked him to take me home first, he still turned under the overpass to a dead end street; obviously he knew this place well, because he went right to it. I asked him where we were going and he said he wanted to talk to me. He turned towards me with that stupid look in his eye and I knew why he had pulled over. He put the car in park and began telling me how pretty I was and that he would not hurt me. He told me I had been doing a great job and he wanted to give me a raise because I had been better than all the other manicurist. I was afraid of him now, but thought of what daddy would tell me to do if he knew where I was... I was nervous because he was a big man and could have easily overpowered me.

When he reached over to touch my hair, that's when I screamed at him and with my bag hit his hand so hard he yelled and I knocked it away from me with all my might. I tried to open the door but he had put the lock on it from the driver's side. I told him that I would tell my daddy and mama if he tried anything and he told me that he knew my mother was not at home with us which shocked me. How could he know where mama was and we didn't even know. He looked me straight in the eye with a smirk and said.

"Your mother and I know each other very well. I see her some Sunday's whether she is sober or not."

I was mortified! Thinking that he knew where Mama was and she had not even contacted me and daddy since she had left. The way he said he knew her made me sick to my stomach.

Even though I did not know where I was at the time, I could see the traffic in the distance and it was still a little daylight left in the sky. Naomi knew she

could have found her way out if she had too. Knowing when to change who you are in time, is very important in life. She remembered the chameleon at Nanas that summer. She finally said to herself, "It is time."

"What?" Mr. Larimer said.

"You are a liar!" She screamed at the man, with such force that it frightened him!

"If you don't let me out of this car you will be sorry!!! Naomi yelled at the top of her voice. Her Daddy had taught her how to fight. He said he wanted her to know how to protect herself. Mr. Larimer looked mad because Naomi had hit him and was unsure about whether she was scared of him or not.

It also shook him up that she had stood up to him and he hurriedly put the car in reverse and backed out of the little dead end street. We did not talk at all until he began to tell me that if I told my daddy I could never work in the town again because everyone went to his church. I told him that I would not say anything to his daughter my dad or the kids at school if he just take me home! He was really nervous now and drove very fast. I prayed we did not wreck. I wanted to make sure I got home since it was already getting dark. Here I had told this big man with big hands and lips to basically buzz off.

As soon as I got out of the car, I took my key and ran it all the way down his car as he drove off. That will be a surprise for him. Who will he say did it?

"Who cares, I thought." Right! My teenage hormones were kicking in fast. Daddy came home and saw me in my room. I told him what had happened and he called Mr. Latimer with the quickness and told him that he would kill him if he ever came near me again. Mr. Larimer told daddy that if he wanted to keep his rank he would be better off sand papering a gorilla's butt than trying to come after him. He was related to daddy's commanding officer. Mr. Latimer said he did not want me in his shop anymore and daddy spoke harshly to him…

"Oh, you don't have to worry about her being in your shop anymore you dirty pervert!" Daddy was furious, but he never said I told you so. That made me feel so much better. Needless to say that ended my working career while I was in school anyway. Daddy was a little upset at first but realized that I had nothing to do with this and did not know enough about life to have seen all that was going on. I didn't even tell him what Mr. Latimer had said about Mama. I never spoke to Beverly again at school.

Daddy would surely have gone and killed him for that. We had a quiet rest of the week in our house. Daddy was frazzled. He had received the final papers to go overseas.

We knew exactly where we were going now and I couldn't wait until we left the states. Finally Daddy cooled down and we had more conversation. I went back to doing extra chores and earning money, but this time it felt good. We were sitting at the breakfast table one morning and there he was, old Mr. Larimer in the newspaper.

He had been charged with multiple counts of molest and rape of all the young girls that had been working in his shop to include his own daughter were cited as victims. He had his daughter picking her virgin school mates for him to hire in the shop and he would attack them. Naomi felt stupid for falling for the lies. Rumor had it that one of the girls became pregnant and Mr. Latimer ended up going to prison for life. As me and daddy read this news, we realized it could have been me in that group. I certainly was prepared to fight that night I thought, not knowing what I would do.

My brain had gone into overdrive. I kept thinking of things that had happened to me where I had to become a different person in order to survive. I realized that needing to change at a moment's notice was important to survival in life. I also reasoned that if I had still been shy, I may have allowed this man to take advantage of me and destroy my childhood if I had not known how to defend myself.

Staying home with her Daddy was the best thing she could have done. Deciding immediately that the answer was "No" in that situation was the best thing she could have done also. Finally Daddy spoke…

"You did well, Honey, I am proud of you!"

"That's right," she recanted.

"I had a good teacher." I did what you taught me to do in a situation. "You always said that depending on your surroundings, you should quickly assess the situation and possibilities and make your move one way or another."

"It was those words daddy, that echoed in my head and I did it and I survived! I love you for teaching me how to defend myself and I'm glad for having the strength to put what I learned to good use. I will always remember this.

"Any unidentified fish is a shark!" We felt sadness for the girls that had been violated by this pervert, but was happy I was not one of the statistics. I agreed to testify against Mr. Latimer because we knew he would lie and someone had to believe those girls. We both sat quietly and daddy threw the newspaper in the recycle bin.

~ CHAPTER 7 ~

The Spiders Web

They say that a spider's web gets stronger when it rains on it. It seemed that my life was changing with each passing year that went by. After that miserable summer with Mr. Latimer, daddy and I went to Germany. We heard through the grapevine that Mr. Latimer committed suicide in prison. Some say someone killed him inside but no one seemed to care. It was very sad. His daughter Beverly ended up going into prostitution. The barbershop closed down and the church was also closed after the investigation showed that the girls at the manicurist station was not all that he had victimized. It was a surreal time for me being out of the country for the very first time and not having mama with us.

There was so much to see in this new and exciting place. The dreams had gotten worse and not being close enough to talk to Nana about them made me sad. She was the only one in the world that knew the torment I felt each time I slept and would wake up. I had to learn how to hide my feelings from Daddy because he had enough on his mind with trying to raise me and make sure I had what I needed. I knew it was lonely not having mama with him, but he pretended not to let it bother him because he didn't want me to see him sad. School in Germany was very different than in the states. I was almost seventeen now and had changed a lot.

Author: Victoria E. Kain

They say that seventeen is supposed to be the time of your life when everything is perfect. All of your girl parts are usually in place and you are not quite an adult but you look and feel like one most of the times. Since I didn't have any siblings, there was nothing to compare myself to. It was just another day for me. I would now be in another country and would have to graduate here not knowing anyone. What a bummer!

We took trips home the first two years we were overseas to see Nana and Grandpa. Grandpa Cody had gotten really sick and we thought we would lose him so Daddy got a hop and we went right away. Grandpa Cody fooled us all and got better and we were very glad. Now they both are doing just fine. Daddy had three more years to go in the military and he would be able to retire. We decided to do his last tour of duty in Germany so that he could take me to all the places he had been without me when he was with mama. He had decided that he would get me into a local college when we got back home so I could be close to Nana and Grandpa Cody and Shellie and Patrice.

He also promised he would buy a new house closer to Nana as well. That was a great gesture but I knew that Daddy was trying to keep me home with him. He wanted to protect me always, but I knew it was time for me to go my own way. There was a feeling I had that kept coming in my heart.
I had made other plans in my mind. Time hurled forward the next years and was now in my last year of school and about to graduate.

Cease To Exist

The timeline for graduation was different in the U.S. and my friends would graduate before I would the same year. Daddy had said that he had a surprise for me which was my graduation gift, but I couldn't imagine what it could be. I hoped it wasn't something really stupid that I couldn't use. Daddy was good for getting goofy gifts for me that he thought were good for me being a girl and all, but they had nothing to do with me actually being a girl. He was still learning and I needed a woman's touch on mater like that. Daddy and I enjoyed our quarters on the base in Germany and it was very comfortable.

We had a live in maid Ms. Earmie who lived with us during the week that stayed with me when Daddy was in the field. She was as old as my baby sitter back home and she even farted while she slept too. We only paid her 30.00 per month and she thought she was rich. I guess for her she was rich. We often thought she was homeless because she never gave us an address for where she lived on the weekend when she wasn't at our place.

At one time I thought she had a crush on Daddy and I used to tease him about that. He threated jokingly that if I didn't stop teasing him about Ms. Earmie, he was going to ask her to marry him and she would become my new mother, and they would have children. We laughed for days about that. Time moved on and daddy and I went everywhere on the weekends.

It was the most beautiful time I can remember in my life. During that summer, my secret was leaked out when I had a bad dream again and Daddy came into my room and woke me up. He said he was afraid for me because when he came in my room I was lying on the floor, reaching for my nightstand. I had to tell him the truth about the dreams I had had for years.

He didn't know what to say but took me to a doctor and they could not find anything wrong. I didn't want him to know about the dreams because he became more protective of me. It still didn't stop us from going places though. He just watched me closer. Soon the time would come for me to graduate. I had made a few friends in Germany, but most of the kids in class were American.

I had gotten everything ready for the graduation and four days before graduation, daddy said that he needed to go to the airport to pick up one of his soldiers that was coming into Germany and he was helping their family get settled. He asked me if I would mind the family staying with us for a few weeks until the soldier got his housing for his family. He even went further and stated that they had a nine month old little girl, knowing how much I loved little babies. He told me that they were bringing the baby with them. Needless to say, I agreed with daddy to help the family out and thought it would be great to have a baby in the house.

Daddy had always been kind to people he met so this was not strange to hear him ask me to support something he wanted to do. I already knew that if he was bringing them into his home he had checked them out thoroughly. He threw in the request for me to ride shot gun with him to the airport…a term he used when we were going somewhere that he wanted company so he wouldn't go to sleep on the road. I would definitely keep him awake.

I didn't mind going but I didn't like riding on the autobahn because they drove so fast on that thing. I hadn't gotten use to that but still agreed to go anyway. We didn't talk much on the way, but when we got to the airport daddy told me to wait in the car. He needed to see if the soldier was in the terminal.

"Okay Daddy," I said, really not caring to get out anyway so I sat in the car sending text messages to Patrice and Shellie wondering what they were doing now. They seemed awfully busy to be out in the country and they hadn't responded back to me. I found that odd because they never have anything to do since they had already graduated. I turned to Pandora on my iPhone and found my station and was listening to that. I figured I would put my headset on so that it would not disturb the baby or the couple once they got in the vehicle. Finally, daddy came out of the terminal and tapped on the window for me to roll it down and I did.

I was searching for the baby that was supposed to be coming with the couple but didn't see a baby or anyone other than people going in and coming out of the terminals.

"Naomi, I want you to meet two of my soldiers," he said very nonchalantly.

"Two, I thought he told me it was one. Maybe the soldier's wife is in the military too."

"Oh well," what difference does it make...I thought. Just when I was about to roll my eyes thinking that some old fuddy duddy would walk up to the window, out through the doors came Patrice and Shellie...I literally threw my phone on the floor and almost knocked daddy down trying to get out of the car door. All three of us were yelling and screaming and jumping up and down like we were kids again. Daddy looked on in sheer joy to see my face light up like a summer sun.

We jumped up and down in unison hugging each other until they had to ask us to move out of the walkway so that people trying to get to their terminals could get through for their flights. Daddy got their two bags and put them in the trunk. I sat in the back this time, on purpose. I wanted to be close to my best friends.

"Daddy, this is the best present you ever could have given me!!!" I said.

"Well, you've been a good sport since your mama left us years ago and you came with me here to Germany.

You have not complained once about anything. Not even that you didn't know anyone like most teenagers would have done. It's amazing! You deserved more than this but I knew you would love to have a gift that wasn't "goofy." So, I wanted to do something for you that I knew you would never forget. Now your friends will be at your graduation and you three can spend your last summer together here in Germany doing what girls do.

It was a great speech, but before daddy could get in the car I jumped up and gave him a big hug and kissed him on the cheek!

"Thank you Daddy!

"Yeah, thank you Mr. Kilpatrick, both Patrice and Shellie told daddy." They had never been out of their little country town since they were born either. So this was a treat for them. It was like being Alice in wonderland. Now my graduation would be complete.

Daddy promised that after graduation, he would take us to Paris, Rome, Venice and Italy. I wondered why he had saved those places for last for us to go to from all the time we had been here in Germany…he was always secretive about things he wanted to surprise me with and he was pretty good at it. All the places that were close by that we normally would not get to see from the U.S., we could go there now and my friends would be with me. This would be the best summer ever and I would never forget it.

Our ride back to our quarters would be a good one and full of chatter. Me, Patrice and Shellie whispered things we didn't want daddy to hear, but knew he had on his bionic ears and was straining to hear what we were saying...when we talked about girl stuff, we took out our pencil and pad and wrote it on the paper...that way it was our secret for sure. We got back to the house and jumped out of the car and ran inside. Daddy was left with the bags to take out as usual. He didn't care as long as I was happy. My neighbor friends looked on as I waved to them and told them we'd be over later and I would introduce my American friends to them. It seemed to be a treat for German kids to meet Americans.

It was cool to know someone from another country. We would have a wonderful summer in Germany. Daddy took us all out to eat that night to this really nice place where lots of kids hung out. Of course daddy stuck out like a sore thumb with only a few parents in there doing exactly what he was doing. They all seemed to nod their heads from across the room, indicating that they were doing the same thing...taking their kids out for a good time.

The day was glorious for us and my friends and I simply could not stop talking. When we settled down for the night, even though we dared not go to sleep and miss any of the gossip that we told each other. We sat on the king sized bed and braided each other's hair. Shellie seemed a little bummed from the long flight.

Neither of them had flown before but Patrice was okay with it. Shellie was having jet lag and wanted to relax. We talked for a long time and believe it or not, Nana had sent me something by her since they lived on the same road. Shellie pulled out a photo album from her bag. I was shocked to see it because Nana had never shown it to me before. Shellie looked at me and confessed.

"I have to tell you, I did peek in the album and looked at all the pictures," she said, smiling a shy grin.

"No you didn't, you are in big trouble," Naomi blurted out making a mad face but changing it as quickly as she made it. She didn't want her friend to think she was angry in any way with her. Shellie was relieved that Naomi was not mad.

"You both can look at the pictures with me if you like," she said. Patrice was busying herself with unpacking and wanted to wash her hair since they were going out the next day. Shellie declined as well since she had already peeked in the album and didn't recognize any of the faces. They left Naomi to look in the album on their own. As Naomi sat on the bed thumbing through the book, she saw many pictures of her mama when she was a little girl. A flood of memories came back to her as she looked at each of the photographs. She saw her Nana when she was really young and she looked to be no more than Naomi's age in the picture.

Everyone looked so young and fresh. There were many pictures that she saw that she didn't recognize and finally, she realized that she didn't see pictures of Grandpa Cody! She saw another man standing with Nana but it didn't dawn on her who this man could have been with her and her mama. She kept looking at the pictures going back and forth and realized that this was a different man in these pictures with Nana and her mama and it was as if they were a family! She continued to search for clues as to this man and finally she saw a wedding picture of her Nana and this same man and realized that Nana had been married once before she married Grandpa Cody. Naomi was confused now wondering if this man was actually her mama's father and not Grandpa Cody.

Naomi looked across the room to where Shellie and Patrice were and they were chattering away in the bathroom like two cackling hens. They paid no attention to her at all. That was just fine with Naomi because she was trying to sort out the pictures in the album she had. She flipped to another page in the back of the album and there was an envelope taped to it. It had begun to yellow from age and she opened it up carefully so as not to disturb the contents and pulled out what appeared to be a birth certificate. As she quickly read the names and details on the certificate, her eyes were like claws grabbing information as fast as she could see it.

This was a birth certificate for a Peggy Louise Fitzgerald which was her mama's maiden name! The odd thing was that the father's name on the birth certificate was "Cody Fitzgerald, but the man Nana was married to was someone else!!! Naomi dropped the book on the bed and looked again to see if the girls were paying any attention to her...they were so absorbed in what they were doing and being in Germany they could have cared less what Naomi was doing and that was a relief for Naomi. She was now trying to put the pieces together of her life and now her Mama's life. "If the man in the picture that was married to Nana was her husband, but she had a child with Grandpa Cody's last name, then what happened here?

Was Nana married and had an affair and had mama? Or, did she have Mama first and then married this man in the wedding photo? Naomi didn't know what to think. She began wondering why her Nana had sent her this information, now, of all times. As she pondered further, she always wondered why her Mama was not close to Nana. She always seemed to keep her distance with her. Even though she loved Nana and Grandpa Cody, there seemed to be a distance there and I never knew what it was and Nana was very hush mouthed about family business. Naomi wasn't sure her Daddy knew any of this but she would share it with him later. She didn't want to spoil her graduation and her friend's vacation that had come to visit her and attend her graduation.

She would look into this more later, but now she tucked the book under her bed where she put everything that she read and joined the girls in the bathroom. There seemed to be many secrets in Naomi's life. Now much of these things were coming to light as she got older. She was beginning to get a strange headache but didn't speak about it. She never wanted to spoil anyone else's good time…she knew how precious that was in life, so she kept quiet about her pain. The three of them had the most fun that night. Laughing and talking and thinking about the future and finally fell asleep. That night, the dream was intense for Naomi. She found herself waking up in the middle of the night with perspiration pouring from her face.

She quickly assessed her friends to see if she had disturbed them but they were both sound asleep but she heard a knock at the door…it was her Daddy…

"Naomi, are you alright honey?" he quietly asked.

"I'm okay Daddy," just a bad dream again.

"Do you need to talk?"

Naomi thought for a moment knowing she was afraid to go back to sleep. She didn't want to wake Shellie and Patrice and accepted her Daddy's invitation. She crawled out of bed and put on her robe and slippers and quietly exited the room with the sleeping girls who were now snoring from their tiresome trip.

Naomi and her Daddy went into the kitchen and her Daddy put some milk in the kettle to heat up for some hot chocolate. He always liked drinking hot chocolate at night. Daddy seemed to never be able to sleep for a full night. Being in the war and all, he had PTSD but had done much better than most soldiers had. I was so thankful that he hadn't lost it having been in the war so long and not having been really injured. Daddy, heated up the chocolate and pulled the kettle off before it could start whistling. That thing would have awakened the dead as loud as it was, but he knew it and grabbed it fast. He poured me a big cup and sat it in front of me. I nestled in on the sofa that was in the living room and he came in and sat down next to me, quickly sipping some of the chocolate making a mustache with the cream on it.

He always wanted to make me laugh when he thought I was sad and it always worked.

"Get over here, girl," you're too far away from me, he said. Trying to make me feel better and to lighten the moment. I scooted over and nestled under his arm and felt safe. It was as if I could talk about my concerns when I was close to daddy so I just let it out.

"Daddy, Nana sent me an album with pictures of Mama when she was a baby."

"Did you know that Nana was married before she was married to Grandpa Cody?" I asked.

"I did."

"Why didn't anyone tell me about it?"

"You were too little honey and that was grown up stuff."

"Well, why am I now being introduced to this grown up stuff?"

"That's because you are now old enough to understand some things Naomi."

"Your Nana told me she was sending you this album when she wrote me weeks after I told her I was sending for Patrice and Shellie to come to your graduation. She wanted you to have the pictures of your Mama so you would remember her always and have them for your family album if you married or if anything ever happened to them.

You know Nana and Grandpa Cody's getting older now. But yes, I knew about Nana's marriage. Naomi hesitated before she asked her next round of questions. She wanted to think about how she would ask the next question and then reasoned that she would just ask. She sipped on the hot chocolate and fired away.

"Well, was Grandpa Cody Mama's father or was it Nana's husband?

Her daddy took a big swallow of hot chocolate as if to clear his throat. He didn't expect Naomi to go there, but knew he had to answer if he had the answer and he did.

"Yes, Grandpa Cody is your Mama's biological father, just like I am yours pumpkin." Daddy said.

He sealed it with a kiss on my forehead. It seemed to make everything better when he treated me like I belonged to him.

He seemed to make everything feel alright with me. I had almost forgot about the dream I had, but my headache was still there. Daddy seemed to know just what to say to make me feel better. Just knowing that Grandpa Cody and Nana were Mama's biological parents, it didn't seem to matter much about the details of anything else. I knew I was growing up because I understood when to let sleeping dogs sleep. I didn't talk about the dream I had had. I felt that what I talked about was enough for the night.

Daddy gulped down all of his chocolate and then drank mine. He ushered me back to bed and reminded me that I had visitors and needed to get some sleep. I went back and got in the bed and it felt good. The girls were still sleeping as I lay there awake for a while and then dozed off again. Morning would come ever too soon. Patrice and Shellie were all messed up on the time change and had to settle down. We talked about our itinerary and decided that we would take a quick French course together since we were going to Paris while they were here.

We took the French course as something fun to do and had a literal blast! They were so shocked at how I had changed but I felt the same way about them too. Patrice had blossomed out and looked amazing. Shellie had long blonde hair and fit perfect in Germany. The guys went crazy over her because she was blonde, but me and Patrice didn't do too badly either.

Patrice and I had all the attention of the older guys 19-21. Of course we couldn't let daddy know this, he would have peeled like a banana. The days we spent together were magnificent. Everything in the city seemed better with my friends with me. It was like having a sister to do things with me. We had been together since we were in kindergarten which we found out was a German word. We explored everything there was to explore and this was the best ending to a beautiful trip.

It was as if Daddy had made memories for me with him in all the places he had been when I was a little girl and couldn't go. My graduation was coming up and I couldn't wait for the day. Patrice and Shellie helped me get ready for it. Daddy took lots of pictures of us before we got to the stadium and everything was beautiful.

I would take another round of pictures with my German classmates so that I would have them in my album from my Germany trip. The ceremony that day was very beautiful. When the music began, there was something that happened to me. I began to feel all grown up, like I was changing in some way. It was as if another part of me was evolving and I had to keep moving forward. I can't explain clearly how I felt but knew that this was a pivotal part of my life and this year had been beautiful. As we all accepted our diplomas, the crowd would be in a frenzy applauding for all the graduates. There would be English signs and German signs congratulating the students and we all tossed our caps in the air at the end like to see it done on T.V.

As I found Daddy and Patrice and Shellie in the crowd, Daddy hugged me and then the girls attacked me with hugs and congratulatory wishes. We all said in unison, "WE ARE FREE FROM SCHOOL!!!" For one moment as we took pictures, I looked around the room and thought I saw Mama sitting in the middle isle. I froze not sure what to think, but was shaken by Daddy telling me to smile for the camera.

My heart was racing just thinking she was there. I also noticed that Daddy's was looking in the same direction I was. 'Could it be?' Did Mama actually come to my graduation and just didn't' have the heart to tell us?' After the pictures were taken I didn't see her anymore. I wasn't sure if it was her anyway and felt that Daddy might have told me if she was coming. Funny thing though…I had wished Mama was there anyway. All kids want both their parents regardless of what the relationship is like. I quickly realized that it made no sense to wish for things that couldn't happen.

I accepted that she wasn't there because she didn't speak to me. She probably wouldn't have smiled on the pictures anyway which would have ruined them for all of us. She never liked Patrice and Shellie either so it was for the best. It still didn't stop me from looking in the audience again as I walked out of the auditorium to go to the car. Daddy said later that someone from back home told him that Mama had said that she was going to Germany to see her daughter graduate.

I never knew for sure, but treasured the thought of believing that she cared enough about me to come and see me. Nothing mattered, anymore. This was the most beautiful three weeks of my life... I would always remember Shellie and Patrice for being there for me. I still could not understand how Mama could not love daddy... he was a wonderful father, to be that, you would have to be a wonderful husband.

Maturity would soon teach me something different about that. The trip finally wound down for Patrice and Shellie. We would take them back to the airport where we picked them up. It was a sad time but I knew I didn't have long before I would be back home with them, so we parted with tears and anticipation of seeing each other again when I returned home.

The next year after Naomi graduated, they left Germany and came back to the United States. Everything was so different. It was amazing how your body and mind adapted to new places and the places where you had been born now seemed foreign. She acclimated to being home once again. Still had the nightmares, but never talking to her daddy about them anymore. She still could not figure out why things kept changing in her mind. Daddy had his own problems and it seemed that more things were happening when we returned home. It didn't really matter now about the dreams that continued to wake me in the night.

I didn't want to burden anyone about what I knew was my problem and I refused to see a shrink. Something told me it was too much to give anyone to try and figure out. The year we came back, Mama finally asked daddy for a divorce. He did not want anything to mar his military career since he had been in so long and was getting out soon so he tried to see her to talk to her about what she wanted from him in the divorce.

He was very quiet about their meeting and didn't say much to me about it. It seemed that she waited right until he was getting out of the military to talk divorce, and we weren't sure if this was strategic or not, knowing he would get great benefits and she would have those too. He knew she wanted to get money from him and he knew that's why she waited, but Daddy didn't care about the money he wanted her to be happy.

I always believed he was still in love with her even though he never said it. He had met a lady in Germany and I don't know how serious that was but he never brought her home to meet me so I took it to be more of a friends with no benefits...well, maybe there were benefits but I just didn't know about it. I remember hearing him talk to this lady on the phone a few times and heard him say something about her coming to the U.S. but he never let me meet her. I think Mama found out about this woman as well. Someone that were mutual friends of theirs I believe were keeping them in the loop of what was going on with both of them.

Author: Victoria E. Kain

This may have been why Daddy never remarried. Lord knows the women in Germany were like ants all over Daddy everywhere we went. Daddy would meet with Mama a couple of times but he never talked about what they discussed and I never asked. Part of me wanted them to get back together and part of me didn't. I remember all the mean things Mama did and didn't know if she would ever be sorry for those things or not. I didn't want to think about my life with her right now since if felt better than it ever did with her. I loved her, but I didn't like her much.

The weeks went by fast and Naomi wanted to go and spend time with Nana since she was back home. She told her daddy that she would be back before nightfall that day and wanted to see Patrice and Shellie. She had gotten her drivers' license in Germany before she left and took the drive out to Nana's and couldn't help but reminisce about when she was a child riding down that same road that seemed to take forever but now was fleeing and more beautiful today than it had ever been.

She reasoned as she passed the old familiar sights, she thought about the Chameleon she saw as a child beside the roadway. It was funny how you travel a road in life and depending on how old you are, that road seems different because you are seeing it from a different mind's eye. When we understand things in life, we can formulate a picture in our mind and connect everything we have ever seen that correlates to it.

Cease To Exist

As an adult, the time was much shorter to drive to Nana's. The old houses now looked very small to her as an adult. The old dirt road was bumpy and uncomfortable. As a child, she never noticed those bumps. When she arrived up on Nana and Grandpa Cody's yard, it was amazing…the house and everything was still the same. Their little house didn't seem smaller like all the houses around it.

The flowers were pretty and she could still smell the honeysuckle. The sun was shining, just the same as when she was a little girl but she was now all grown up. Naomi, couldn't help but look around as she leaned out of the car window. It was as if she wanted to soak up this beautiful scenery that had encapsulated her as a child.

There was still something very strange and special about her Nana's house where she had grown up. She finally opened the car door and stepped out on the grass which was greener than she had ever seen it before. She slowly closed the door and when she turned around, Nana and Grandpa Cody were miraculously standing on the front porch like they stood when she was a child. They stood there frozen like statues, just staring at her. It was a strange feeling she got today that she had never had before. She was happy to see them since she had been gone a few years, but finally Naomi realized it looked as if her grandparent's had not aged a day since she had been gone. She hurried over to them to give them a hug and to see if what she was seeing was real, and it was.

Author: Victoria E. Kain

They hugged her Grandpa Cody gave her a big hug which he usually is shy about doing. But, today he did. Then Nana spoke first.

"Baby," she said.

"Don't you look pretty, just like your Mama did when she was your age?" She was looking off towards the window as if to think about old memories of her and Mama. Things must have been really bad for Nana and Mama. They never told me what happened but with the pictures I had, I put two and two together.

"You look good too Nana." I said, trying to make her feel good as I walked up on the porch and made a beeline for the swing.

"Oh, stop telling your tales," she said, smiling at me. Time wasn't taking a toll on Nana. She was as perky as she used to be when I was little and she walked just as straight as I was walking. Grandpa Cody went on around to the back of the house. No one ever knows why he stayed in the back so much, but Nana and I on the old swing like we use to when I was little.

"Lord have mercy!" she said.

"My old bones aren't what they use to be."

"Mine either Nana." Naomi quickly responded as she smiled and rubbed her long smooth legs. Before the conversation could go any further, she did what she always did when she came to the old house. She inspected it. She jumped up and took her walk through the house like always.

Cease To Exist

Everything was exactly the same as if time had stood still on the old farm. I loved the smell of the lilacs that grew on the side of the house and the honeysuckle. The kitchen was still the same as well. The old wood burning stove and the wood box on the floor beside it. The wash basin was still in the same place and the soap was still on the side of it. When Naomi looked at the wash basin that almost sent her into shock that summer when she had too much soap in eyes, she seemed to have a flash of light go through her. Her mind raced back to a time when she was home with her mama and there was an argument going on between her and her Daddy. Naomi quickly shook herself and brought her thoughts back to the present. She felt as if she had been dreaming and looked outside the window and it seemed that the sun was still shinning.

She didn't understand what had happened but realized that what had just happened felt like what she experienced in the dreams she had that taunted her each night. Naomi left the little kitchen and went back to the porch and talked for a while until Nana was visibly tired. They caught up on all the things that had happened while she was gone and Naomi finally picked up her phone and called Patrice first since she was the closest to Nana's house and told her she was there. A call was placed to Shellie's and she did not get an answer but left her a message.

Author: Victoria E. Kain

Patrice hurried down the long driveway that joined with Nana's and ran to the house like a 10 year old. I could still see her leaving her house since it was between some of the trees that had grown up in Nana's front yard. The properties were side by side not even a block away. Nana got up to go in the house to lie down while my friend and I caught up on our lives.

As she walked in the house, I looked back at her as I waited in the yard for Patrice and Nana's silhouette seemed to disappear into the old house like Ms. Amy's did that day we took the buttermilk to her. It was a weird feeling, but I turned my attention back to Patrice who was now coming onto the yard. Patrice was the only one that came down to the house that day. She walked on the porch looking as beautiful as ever. We talked and hugged each other remembering how much we enjoyed our summer in Germany.

We talked about the guys we met in Germany that we kept in touch with, unbeknownst to Daddy and discussed our limited dating experiences. Daddy still wouldn't allow me to date. Patrice had decided not to become a doctor and I hadn't decided what I wanted to major in in college. Before we began talking about our life I was concerned that Shellie didn't answer. I could see her folk's car in the yard but didn't see the kids or Shellie.

"Where is Shellie?" I asked, flicking Patrice's hair because it was now longer than mine.

"Well, Patrice said.

"I know what a cry baby you are and I don't want to spoil our day."

"No I'm not a cry baby, where is she…don't tell me she's pregnant or something? You know we all agreed to have our babies at the same time."

"No, she's not pregnant and you are too a cry baby!"

"Just get to it…it can't be that bad," Naomi chimed in with a bit of sarcasm. Even with the sarcasm, she searched Patrice's face to see if it was really something bad. Finally, realizing there was something that was going on she asked again, but this time in a different more concerned tone.

"Really, Patrice, is it something bad?" Naomi stated. Now with a more serious empathetic look on her face.

"Well, it is," Patrice responded. She told Naomi to brace herself for what she was about to tell her.

"Okay, you see…she stumbled on her words. "Shellie didn't come because she had a situation at her home last summer when we returned from Germany. We didn't want to write you about it and asked your Nana and Grandpa not to tell you because we didn't want to ruin a beautiful summer we had. Naomi was really worried now thinking Shellie was dead! Naomi insisted,

"Tell me what is wrong with Patrice!!!"

"I want to know," she demanded! We both could tell that we had grown up.

Cease To Exist

As young girls, we would never have been this demanding of one another but Naomi was almost shaking knowing something had happened to her friend. Patrice began to tell what happened…

"Well, Shellie and I had a wonderful time with you in Germany." On the way home, we took a billion pictures on the plane with strangers because we were so amped up about being able to say we had finally left the country and actually travelled somewhere else. We became famous that year with all our friends here. Shellie had even said that she no longer had to lie about having been somewhere during the summer because the kids use to always tease her about that." Patrice was fidgeting now but continued.

"After we got home and everything seemed to be getting back to normal. Things began to get worse with Shellie's mom and dad.
"I knew they always had some issues in their relationship," Naomi said, but who hasn't. "As you saw with my parents."
"Now they are divorcing and it will be finalized soon."
"Well, it is much worse that than Naomi," Patrice said with a very sad look on her face.
"What happened?" Naomi asked, now very anxious.
"Well, it was right after the kids had gotten out of school one evening and some of the kids from the Mahoney farm had come down to play with Shellie's little brothers and sisters Betty Lee and Lionel that afternoon.

Cease To Exist

They all ran around the house playing hop scotch and jump rope like kids normally do." Shellie had hurried to get the breakfast dishes done before her daddy was to come home because he had been gone for days now but that wasn't unusual and her mother had been sick about it. They were having really bad times and she stayed in bed a lot crying. Shellie being the oldest, always tried to look after the kids during this time because of her mother's state of mind.

The little Mahoney kids came into the house and were hungry because they didn't have food at home. Shellie gave them all biscuits, ham and jelly for breakfast. It seemed as if they never stopped eating jelly and bread from the time I have known them. Not that it is bad, Patrice said, making sure she didn't come off as being better than Shellie but added...but even "we" moved up at some point when daddy got a promotion at the Mill. Shellie's family always continued to struggle down to the end.

The kids hurried and ate and didn't leave a morsel of food on their plates; they longed to ask for the scraps but were too excited to see their friends and ran back outside to play. They would not have to play while they were hungry and that was probably the reason their mother let them come down to Shellie's house at all that early in the day.

Author: Victoria E. Kain

Cease To Exist

Seeing the kids was important but getting those biscuits was even more important. Shellie's mom finally got out of bed that day and sat at the entrance of the open door of the little house listening to the kids laugh and giggle outside playing. They never had much but always seemed to be happy even thought their parents had a rough time. Shellie's mom smiled a longing smile, remembering better days as if she wanted to be a child again herself.

Times had been hard but this was the worst for her. She sat there in the doorway in a tattered dress, never having money to buy a new one. Today she was chaperoning the kids making sure they were honest in their game rules. She finally got up to help Shellie do the chores she normally would have done and to try to get out of the depressed mode she had been thrust into by the situation with her husband. She loved him so much, but he would beat her and leave home and be gone for days. It had been this way ever since they were forced to get married because she was pregnant with Shellie who was the oldest.

Then she went in to make up the beds. Shellie told me that her mom looked at her and said to her. "Well, I guess he's gone for good this time Shellie. Shellie told her Mama, you don't know that for sure, he might come back; you know how daddy is sometimes."

Cease To Exist

He always liked to roam the streets. "Yeah, honey, but you don't know how your daddy has hurt me this time." Shellie's mom lifted up her skirt to reveal her upper thigh and she gasps when *she saw huge black and blue bruises on her legs. Shellie began to cry out.* "Mama, good riddance if he has to beat you like this!!!" *No one should have to take this! Her mother agreed but told her not to worry that they would be alright.* "I promise you I will hurt a man if he tries to hurt me or my children if I marry." *I mean it Mama!* Shellie had told her mother.

Reluctantly, Patrice went on to finish telling Naomi what happened that summer... *"They both just finished up the chores and began to sit around the old table and shell the peas they would have for dinner. As they prepared the stove to cook, Shellie's mom called her son in to get wood from the wood pile. Soon the kitchen was aglow with food cooking. Shellie told me, they wanted to have a celebration meal that evening since they reasoned that their father was not coming back.*

No more hiding in the dark of night on the weekend when he would get drunk and shoot his gun in the old farm house. He could have easily killed any of them by mistake. Shellie had also told me that she was very sad for her mother. That day Shellie said that her younger brother, who was only a few years younger than she was, was sent to the store to get sodas for dinner.

Author: Victoria E. Kain

Cease To Exist

It was a splurge they would have because it was important to let the children feel good even though their daddy was never coming back. Shellie's mom warned her son to check for the traffic before crossing the highway because it was a major road. They didn't live far from the store but still it was off the main highway. As they waited for dinner and for their brother to return, the children ran to the door yelling in excitement.

"It's daddy, its daddy!" They cried out. Shellie and her mom looked at each other and hurried to the door drying their hands on their soiled aprons. "See Mama, I told you he would be back!" Even Shellie was excited. Shellie's mom was in disbelief. Shellie said her daddy came up to the door, wearing his Sunday clothes as if he was someone special coming to visit."
"James, Shellie's mother said," calling her husband's name with a nervous anticipation of whether he was staying or not. "I just came for the rest of my things, now!

I don't want no trouble out of you!" Shellie's Mama was sad all over again. Her hopes of him coming back were shot down. Shellie said she could see the pain in her mother's eyes as she hobbled behind him. Shellie *couldn't take it anymore and remembered her mother's bruises. She did what her mother did not have the courage to do. Shellie told her dad to get his things and go! "Just leave us alone!!! She screamed at him for the first time in her life.*

Today, she had no respect for the man that brought her into the world that was now crushing them all."

"Girl, you don't talk to me like that, I'm your daddy!" He exclaimed.

"Well, apparently not for long! I don't need a daddy! Gone and leave us alone! Shellie yelled to him, having lost all respect for the man she once loved. Her mother was crying and began begging him not to leave again as he got his things and threw them in a paper bag. The kids stopped playing outside and were told to go back in the house. Shellie's mom didn't want them to see him leave them and sent all the children in the house to include the ones that were visiting.

Shellie's mother then walked behind her husband tugging at his shirt and he was pushing her away, fanning her like she was a fly or an aggravating gnat that he wanted away from him. As he crossed the highway one last time, she followed him yelling and crying.

"What are we going to do without you James?"

"I can't take care of all these babies by myself!!!"

"What are we to do???" Shellie's mother was almost out of control with sadness. Of all things that day, Shellie's father had decided to park his car across the busy highway instead of on the yard where he normally did. It was as if he was letting everyone know that he was simply a visitor that day and not a resident.

Cease To Exist

As he walked towards his car, his wife followed him crying and pleading for him to stay and asking him how she would provide for all of the children with him gone.

He cursed his wife and turned his back to her as he walked across the highway. They argued only for a moment more as he told her, "I am never coming back to you or these kids again!" NEVER!!! He yelled. Soon, he would eat his words and life would never be the same again for anyone on that road today. As his fatal words echoed in the air on that summer day, he got ready to open the door to get in his vehicle as he pushed his wife to the ground, soon they saw the massive truck coming down the highway and thought nothing of it.

They continued to exchange horrible words and finally without even looking back, they felt the wind move across their faces like a cool breeze from the fast moving truck. Soon of nowhere, they heard the screeching of all eighteen tires on the massive truck as it scraped the highway on the hot asphalt. Smoke was now coming from the engine as the driver desperately tried to stop the vehicle. Shellie's mom and dad's insults halted as they focused their attention on the truck while they both were stunned by the unusual commotion and still did not realize what has happened.

Cease To Exist

As the truck driver was desperately trying to come to a complete stop to keep from jack knifing, Shellie's parents looked over to a section of the highway on the edge of the road in the brushes. It was as if something prompted them to look for the reason the driver of the truck was stopping in such a dangerous fashion.

They finally saw a faint dark spot on the roadway. Still, not realizing what it was, they became afraid thinking the driver may have had a heart attack or a stroke while trying to stop the vehicle. Instinctively, they hurried to the vehicle to see if the driver needed help which halted their arguing. They knew that many times rabbits or sometimes a deer might cross the road but they didn't see anything that looked like an animal.

As they came closer to the spot on the highway, they could see the dark red blood from something that had been hit but could not see where it was. They thought the driver was stopping to check to see what he may have hit and to remove the remains off the road. As Shellie's parents got closer, the children came out on the porch to see what was happening along with their parents. They didn't leave the porch because they had been taught never to cross the highway without adult supervision.

Author: Victoria E. Kain

Cease To Exist

They finally saw the driver's door opening and the man dropped out of the cab, falling to the ground like a drunk man, shaking and trembling. He unsteadily walked over to the side of the highway before Shellie's parents could get to him. He was looking over in the ditch wading through the bushes as if he has lost something of great value. It was not uncommon for snakes to be laying in brush that high, but the man continued to wade with his arms flailing back and forth like an uncontrolled machete. He didn't seem to care what happened to him.

Whatever he was searching for was important enough for him to risk his life. Soon, it was apparent that he had found what he was looking for. He dropped to his knees in the bushes which almost covered him from view and began wailing violent uncontrollable tears. Raising his hands to the sky, he groaned, "My God! My God,' what is this I have done!!! "Oh, God, please forgive me!!!" Shellie's mother begin to look back at her children standing on the porch in a huddle after hearing the man praying for forgiveness.

As her motherly instinct were kicking in, still not knowing why the man is so distraught, she and her husband finally reached the driver Her husband was trailing behind her now in a slow motion trot. When Shellie's mother finally turned her attention to the man… She boldly asked the man a sobering question.

"Mister, are you okay?" she asked.

The man is not able to speak for crying so hard. She demands again an answer, this time with more emphasis; as if to try to snap him out of this panic he is in.

"Are you alright, Mister??? " Finally he screams.

"Nooooooo!!!! He screamed and points to the ground where he stood.

Shellie's mother slowly turned her attention to where the man was pointing and there in a lifeless heap… lay their five year old sons tiny body, grossly mangled on *the side of the road in the ditch. They could see parts of his clothing on the bushes where the force had disrobed him. He lay almost in a fetal position as if he were merely asleep. Shellie's mother faints at the sight of her child laying there and the father got to her and slumped down to the ground in horror and began weeping together.*

The children on the porch to include Shellie began wailing, not knowing what their parents had seen. The sheer fact that their parents were distraught caused them to feel the pain as well. Their five year old son had been crying and running behind his mother pleading with her for his father to stay as they crossed the highway. Her baby brother was struck by the oncoming truck and killed instantly. His love for his father and mother had caused his life to be innocently taken. It was the saddest day of their life that day, and it made her father a liar. Needless to say, Shellie's dad never left.

He stayed there with the family but Shellie was not able to function after that. The family was never the same again. Shellie would cry when her father would get drunk after that. She would say that she wished that she could go where her little brother was to escape the pain and misery of their life.

Naomi remembered what her Nanna had told her as a little girl about the Chameleon. She remembered that it was sort of like the wanting or needing to change in a difficult situation and if you didn't, you could be lost forever like the chameleon that was on the side of the road... "gone forever." The children on that old road were never the same again after that. It seemed that no one smiled anymore. Shellie never got over the way she lost her little brother and why he had died so young. Their poverty never ended but their father never left them... at least not physically.

Even though the driver was not charged for the accident because the child walked into the roadway, he owned the trucking company and offered to pay for the funeral expenses for the child. He also heard about what was happening when the accident occurred and how the parents had been arguing which caused the child to follow his mother to his death. He felt pained for the family and he paid off the deed for the old house where Shellie's family had been paying on for years. He put the deed in Shellie's name so they would always have a home because he said that Shellie's mother was not stable mentally.

Cease To Exist

It became the first thing they ever owned. Patrice finished her sad account of Shellie and Naomi didn't know what to say after Patrice told her this horrifying story about their dear friend. Such a beautiful summer they had in Germany just months earlier before the tragedy. Life was strange. One minute, things were great…the next, tragedy could take you for a long one way journey. It was unimaginable. Naomi burst into a floodgate of tears. She struck her fist on the arm of the swing over and over trying to pound out the pain she felt. She only wished she could find Shellie and help her through this dire situation.

Patrice continued to fill Naomi in on other happenings in the area since she had been gone. But nothing was more tragic than that. Old Ms. Amy had died but she was well in her 90's and had lived a long life. It wasn't that it was okay that her life was lost, it was just that it wasn't snuffed out of her like Shellie's brothers' life was at only 5 years old. He had not even lived yet.

"Shellie's parents had been going through some pretty tough times Naomi." Patrice said. Naomi was still silent. Patrice wanted to try to soothe Naomi's pain for their friend but couldn't. Patrice had almost gotten over it, but understood what it felt like to hear the news for the first time.

"They were constantly fighting Naomi."

"Every Saturday night their father would get drunk and come in the house with his gun threatening to shoot his wife and the kids.

"We would hear gunshots down the road and my papa would say, 'Junior is drinking that liquor again.' He would tell us to stay away from the windows in case he did shoot and a stray bullet came our way. He was going to kill somebody by accident one day if he didn't stop drinking." People thought it was a way for him to deal with his own grief of losing his son knowing he was the cause of his death.

If only he had parked his car in the yard like he should have, the child never would have entered the roadway." Naomi sat quietly and cried…she couldn't talk any more about the situation. Patrice was right, she was a tear bag and she couldn't help it. This was a lot to digest and she hated for anyone to be in pain. This was too much to bear.

"She vowed she would never let a man beat her or take advantage of her. Even though they wanted to console Shellie, but no one knew where she was. It was said that Shellie was sent away from home. She wanted to kill her father when he would drink. She reasoned that there was not much left for them. It was best that she leave because her mother still loved her father and allowed him to abuse her. We haven't heard from her since then. So I don't know where Shellie is and no one will tell us." Patrice and Naomi were quiet. They sat on the front porch in the swing together and slowly rocked themselves back and forth as if to soothe their broken hearts for Shellie. They prayed silently for the family and for themselves.

Patrice left after a little while longer and Naomi went inside and decided to stay the night with Nana. She didn't want to go home feeling the way she did. She called her daddy and told him she would be home in the morning. Nana was just fine with that. She didn't mind her staying at all.

Nana cooked Naomi's favorite supper but she didn't eat much. Soon she got ready for bed that night and would not rest at all. The once comfortable bed she slept in as a child now seemed very small and cramped in comparison to how she felt in it as a little girl. She knew she was only there for a few days and would be leaving the next week for college, so staying with Nana was a good thing for her. She would absorb all the memories and take them with her. Her childhood would be memorialized and sealed once and for all. She was entering adulthood now and there was no turning back.

She went to bed that night at Nana's and time seemed to stand still. She knew she was leaving the next morning to go home and would pack for her trip to school in a small town in New York. It would be a new experience for her, but in light of this news about Shellie, she knew it was time for a change in her life. There was something strange about her sleep that night. Her dream was not as intense as it had been in the past. It seemed that the pain she was already in was causing her dream to subside.

She slept the entire night. When she awakened the next morning to leave. She woke up early and Nana and Grandpa Cody were already awake. They both hugged and kissed her goodbye and wished her well. When she arrived home, her Daddy met her at the door and gave her a big hug. "What was that for?" Naomi asked her dad, all the while sucking it up like a sponge.

"I missed you Pumpkin," that's all, her daddy said.

"I missed you too Daddy."

They didn't talk much after she got back that day, but she did find out that he had gotten the divorce papers in the mail from Mama.

That's probably why he was very emotional and wanted to be close. He also said he was not sure what Mama really wanted to do. She had been trying to contact him before she sent the papers but daddy wasn't responding the way she thought he should. She had lost some weight from what I had heard and probably thought daddy would be turned on by that but it didn't work.

He seemed unsure of what he wanted to do also. I really didn't care what they did at this point. I knew I was an adult and had to make decisions for myself. The week would move by swiftly and I had finally gotten Daddy's approval for school. I was leaving anyway but wanted him to say to me that it was okay and he finally did. The day came for me to leave for school and daddy did something I never expected. He stood in the doorway with me and broke down crying…I don't mean small weeping, he really bawled!

Cease To Exist

It frightened me at first and when I asked him why such hard tears, what he said next broke my heart and I knew I'd have to leave quickly or I would cancel my trip.

"I love you Naomi! You are all I have in this world and now you are leaving me!" he said, weeping.

It was the hardest thing for me to accept from a man who had loved me all my life and gone to war three times and survived. Now, to come home and lose his wife that he loved and then lose the only person he really knew loved him.

To see him break down like a baby was a lot for me to take in. I couldn't help myself. I joined him in the tears until it was clear that one of us had to stop. I stepped up to the plate and did it...I told daddy it was time for me to go and he finally let me go. I believe I was the last piece of Mama that he had in me and now I was leaving him.

I got in the car as he watched me pull out of the driveway onto the road. He waved and threw a kiss at me. I caught it and held it to my heart and pulled off. Instinctively, I looked back at the house. Daddy, looked as if he faded into the house. The house looked lonely and desolate. It reminded me of Ms. Amy when she used to walk into her house when we would take her some milk. She would disappear in the dark opening as if something just swallowed her up and she would vanish out of sight.

Author: Victoria E. Kain

Cease To Exist

The trip was long and arduous, but I got to New York safely in one piece. Soon I would get settled into my new apartment. The trip was sobering for Naomi. Even though New York was a big city and not too far away from where she lived, she still longed for that country atmosphere that made her feel at home. She found a small town on the outskirts of the city that had all the old charm of her home town.

She had been accepted in a four year college there in the small town of Perrington, and would make this her temporary home and try to forget all the tragedy she had experienced in her life. She even hoped the dreams would stop since there would be nothing to trigger them. That thought would be short lived in her new surroundings. The location reminded her a lot of her home as it seemed to be in the middle of nowhere, but it was one of the most beautiful places she had ever seen.

Everybody in this town seemed to know each other which seemed to made life good for the residents here. She hoped it would be the same for her. The old shops were on a beautiful tree lined street and strangely enough many old people walked about as if they were just hitting the prime of their lives like in her home town back in Canoga. It was almost exactly the same as her home town. It was an eerie feeling that came over her as if she had experienced this feeling before.

She dismissed the thought, trying not to send her mind in the vortex of her past memories. She truly wanted to start a new life not knowing what was about to happen to her. The good thing was that there seemed to be very few children on the main streets.

Most of them were riding their bikes quietly down the side streets and made the town look like a Norman Rockwell scene from one of his oil paintings.

Naomi was soothed by the shear relaxed atmosphere of this town and hoped it would be good for her to settle here for a while. The scenery was soothing and people seemed to be happy. Some were tourist and were probably there to break the monotony of their hectic lives in the big city. When all was said and done, it appeared that this little town would be a good place to start life over for Naomi.

Naomi was hopeful that she would be able to have a new beginning. She would try to put her past behind her but, sadly, the depth of sadness in her life would soon bleed into her hopeful future, causing her to take a turn for the worst. This life she was beginning would soon be short lived.

Today, as she strolled down the one-way streets, she stopped to peer into the windows of the pretty dress shops and bakery's.

Knowing she had no extra money to buy anything right now, she still treasured the idea of simply "window shopping." It made her feel alive for the first time in her life. As if she were free to do whatever she dreamed of doing. She in-conspicuously watched the people scurry from store to store, wondering if she could ever be as complacent and happy in her own life as these people seemed to be.

As she watched the couples holding hands whispering to each other, she tried to remember what it felt like to have someone special in her life. She couldn't recall a moment as such, but dismissed the idea. Her thoughts were quieted for a moment as she stopped at an outside café and took a seat. "No one can be this content," she thought. As she continued watching the people around her as if they were perfect. She continued pondering her surroundings soaking in the scenery for the day while she acclimated herself to her new home. Naomi was always a daydreamer.

It was how she had survived her childhood with her mother. What better time than now, to daydream about what she observed? She knew that everyone had a story to tell but most are simply too weak to tell it, or not brave enough to re-live the sordid details of events long enough to write the memories down on paper to resolve their issues.

Cease To Exist

How frightening it would be if the world knew my intimate thoughts? She pondered. To see me in a compromised position, with no way to escape would be tragic, she thought...Yet, many of us face this dilemma every day of our lives. Some of us are verbally abused. Some mentally or sexually abused. Some battered, scorned or abandoned. Some put down for what others feel they do not possess. Some because of the color of their skin or the length of their hair or simply because you may not be as educated to the same degree as others and some...simply because they are born.

Naomi continued to think about many things as she sat waiting for a waitress to come to her table and take her order...she felt she would prefer not to divulge her intimate secrets to total strangers and would always be private. This meant she would choose to endure the misery of her personal issue alone and it would continue to fester within her. She would keep everything in her head only to relive every sordid detail of events that had taken place over and over again in her life. Finally a waitress approached her table interrupting her inward thoughts.

"What will you have today Ma'am?"

"I will have the corned beef on rye with pickles, mustard and tomato's and a garden salad or steamed Broccoli." The waitress, never looked up and continued writing...

"Will that be all?" she finally asked popping her gum.

"Oh, also an unsweetened green tea."

Author: Victoria E. Kain

Cease To Exist

The waitress finished the order and before she could pick up the menu and leave the table, Naomi noticed that the waitresses name was the same as one of her high school friends, Jennifer Kate. She knew her very well and Jennifer was on the Cheerleading Squad from her old high school. She had known her since the 6ᵗʰ grade but she still wasn't sure…She hesitated at the thought of taking the conversation from giving her food order to this stranger to asking this woman if she was someone from her old high school.

It was the oddest thing…this woman looked so much like the girl from school it would be a spooky moment if it wasn't her. 'Could it be Jennifer?' she thought briefly. 'People do change over the years.' Her thoughts were going haywire with the foggy notion that this could be the Jennifer she knew. Their family had left the area after that last year in high school, so it could be her. Finally she decided to take a chance and approach the waitress.

"Excuse me Miss, your name is the same as my high school girlfriend." "You wouldn't happen to have graduated from Windstorm High school would you?"

"Oh, you must be new around here"…the waitress responded.

"This name is as old as the concrete on this walk-way.

"Everyone knows the name "Jennifer" was my great grandmother's name and we have lived her for centuries in this town. My mother stuck it on me and made me swear never to change it before she died. Sooo, I am stuck with it…She smiled a matter-o-fact side smile.

"And to answer your question, "no," I graduated overseas, Army brat. You know how that is!"

"You must be new in town?" she asked, popping her gum and tiding up the table while she chatted.

"Yes I am," Naomi replied.

"Well, where are you from?"

Naomi stopped for a moment as if to think about the answer. She had drawn a complete blank and couldn't figure out why her memory was gone about where she was from. The familiar place where she grew up. She further didn't understand why her heart was racing with that question and didn't know whether she should speak at all.

It was the scariest moment she had encountered. What was happening to her? She seemed stressed and the waitress picked up vibes on her tension and finally spoke. Naomi's hesitation caused the waitress to wonder if she had been too personal and she quickly responded.

"Well, welcome to Little New York, where everyone is family! I will get your order." 'What do you know,' Naomi thought. Totally dismissing the waitress leaving her table. The statement "where everyone is family," caught her attention and seemed to bring her back to a reality.

It was what folks back home used to say to visitors when they came through the town. It was like a light bulb came back on. Naomi seemed to come back to her senses and she could see the waitress in the open kitchen talking to the cook and looking her way. She smiled as if the conversation she had had with Naomi had been a waste of time. Naomi was a bit embarrassed and couldn't understand why she couldn't remember where she was from…that was odd.

Her memory seemed to completely fail her for no reason. She had also begun to perspire out of the blue. Why had it been so difficult to answer a simple questions? She always relished in the idea of remembering positive times she had encountered in her life and being able to share that moment with others always gave her joy. She didn't know what had caused her brain to consume itself with details of misery at this time?

So much, that she forgot who she was and where she was from. It was as if something was preventing her from taking that one small moment to feel good about herself and the new life she was beginning. The unfortunate thing was that Naomi was holding on to some toxic baggage she had experienced which was causing her to become weighed down.

It was like a ship covered with barnacles on its hull. Everyone knows that if there are enough barnacles on a ship, soon, it would silent, but swiftly go down in the deepest part of the ocean never to be seen or heard of again. Naomi didn't want that…The dreams she had as a child had never gone away either. As she sat starring at the people walking by the restaurant, she wondered what each of them were saying to the people they were walking with.

She kept watching the cook in the open kitchen across the counter where she sat by the open door. The cook seemed angry about something and his mannerism was that of someone who didn't want to be there. They were slinging utensils and food and she wondered if it was her order that was being prepared with such vengeance. Naomi watched the waitress going from table to table with her tiny little waistline that looked so neat in the pink uniform she wore. Her hair was long and pretty.

She had it in a simple pony tail but it was shiny and healthy like Naomi's use to be before. Naomi wished she had not cut hers so short, but knew it would grow back fast. She was determined to have a better conversation with the waitress when she returned with meal. Naomi, continued observing the waitress as she systematically smiled at the customers.

She noticed that she smiled more at the men rather than the women…'humph,' Naomi thought, she seems to always make eye contact with the males at the table first when she has a couple. That was interesting to notice. She scratched her head and wondered if the waitress's life could be as happy as she made it appear to be. After all, waitressing was not a glamourous job. No one's life is that good all the time. Naomi thought about all the things that had been hidden from her as a child.

The fact that Nana had been married before she married Grandpa Cody. She only found out about this after she was graduating High school. How often do our lives stay hidden from the world? Each of us have our own story to tell but she wondered what the waitress's story would sound like. 'Would this be her first friend in New York? Could it be?' After all, they were about the same age… maybe? She thought. Naomi always wanted to make others laugh or feel better about themselves.

When she was not soothing someone else's wounds, she would sit quietly in a corner and bind her own…some of those were even inflicted upon her by the ones she tried to help. She could never figure out why she lived her life helping others learn how not to fear, yet fear was always her personal bedfellow. The nightmares were becoming worse now. She was getting to the point that she was afraid to go to sleep thinking she would never wake up.

During the dreams, something always seemed to wake her up and stop the pain. Naomi finally stopped daydreaming as the waitress came back to the table with her meal.

"Well, here you go," she said, placing each plate on the table one by one.

"Corned Beef on Rye, a salad and it comes with muddy puddles, which is what we call mashed potatoes and gravy around here..., steamed broccoli, green tea and... did you order the apple pie?"

"No, I didn't!" Naomi quickly responded.

"I need to lose a few pounds and shouldn't even look at these Muddy things you brought."

They both laughed and the waitress lamented.

"Here, here, now...I know exactly what you mean!" She positioned the tea on the table in front of Naomi and was about to leave...

"Enjoy your meal!"

Naomi, hesitated for a moment but realized it was her last chance to do something she had not done before which was to reach out to someone else for companionship. She knew she only had two best friends in the whole world and now one was missing. She needed to open up more. She wanted to do new things in this new place where she would be for the next four years.

"Well, I could enjoy it a lot more if I did not have to eat alone!"...At that moment, to Naomi's surprise, the waitress responded in kind.

Cease To Exist

"Well, normally we don't do this, but I like you for some reason and I am about to go on my break for the evening and get a bite, if you don't mind, I could sit here with you." Naomi was shocked at the bold response, and quickly accepted the offer.

"That would be great!!!"

"The only thing though, the waitress said, I will tell my boss you are my cousin. That way, they don't think I am gay or something. They also have a "no fraternizing policy."

They both laughed and made a funny face as they watched the cook snatch off his apron and walk to the back of the tiny restaurant. The waitress went and picked up her meal and brought it back to the table. It was a simple order of fries and a hamburger...

"Is that all you are eating?" Naomi asked,

"Yep, this is enough!" Jennifer added abruptly.

"I can't gain any more weight either...my boss doesn't want fat waitresses, if you know what I mean."

Naomi, smiled reluctantly but didn't quite get it...she noticed the way her boss kept looking towards their table, but Jennifer ignored him. It was as if she had some kind of invisible control over him. There was a sense of authority she had and it was obvious. She didn't seem afraid to be sitting with a customer and took a big bite out of the hamburger and looked at Naomi and made small talk.

"So…where are you from?" she asked, downing the burger like a lumberjack. The questions was a repeat of what she had asked Naomi earlier in their meeting and she hadn't answered her. It seemed that she wanted to ask it again and this time commanded an answer because of her invitation.

Naomi started to take a bite of her potatoes and began to speak.
"Well, if I am going to tell you where I am from, I might as well start from the beginning…
"Why don't you do that," Jennifer said, downing the fries now.
"I have a whole hour for lunch!"
Naomi smiled, feeling a sense of accomplishment in her first encounter with a stranger in the little big city. She began her conversation as if she were making a confession…as a joke. There was something strange about being there with Jennifer.
It was as if she already knew her but didn't know why she felt that way.

She couldn't believe she was telling this story again and it didn't feel right that she was repeating herself in one day as if something else was compelling her to keep talking about herself over and over again. She stopped being concerned about this thought and just started talking again.

Author: Victoria E. Kain

Cease To Exist

"Well, I am Naomi Kilpatrick and I grew up in a small town like this one but only more in the country setting and not the city. I had a mother and father like most people, but my parents were an interracial couple and my mother didn't love my dad and she didn't like me much either because I looked a lot like him. But the good thing is he loved me dearly."

She couldn't believe she was spewing all of her life history out to this stranger like this. "I ended up moving to this city like most people trying to get away from my past. I know that there will be all sorts of things that will come from moving too fast or not fast enough but I want to know more about myself. I was a very shy young girl. I had pigtails, freckles and long curly hair…obviously I have regressed and cut it all off."

Naomi ran her hands through her hair holding it out to the side to let Jennifer see how short she had cut it. My Nana also loved me very much too. I really miss her. She was like the mother I didn't have. Naomi continued chattering about her life…she had completely stopped trying to figure out why she was telling this stranger all these things. Finally she stopped talking and the bewildered waitress spoke.

"Wow," your grandmother sounds like she adored you." Taking another bite of her fries, looking at Naomi with a faraway look in her eyes.
"Yes, she did."

Naomi put her fork down and continued talking with Jennifer. She took a sip of her tea and looked longingly out of the window for a moment as if she were wishing she had her Nana here with her. She couldn't let go of that memory because it always kept her in a comfortable place in her soul. She loved remembering everything about her Nana. Believing it was the only real thing she ever had next to her Daddy. It was as if her parents were in the background of her life and Nana was in the center.

She went on to tell the story again to her new found friend. "Although I was the youngest of three siblings and the only one left at home, I was never permitted to go any further than home and to my Nana's house every summer after my brothers went off to college and one to the Army.

"I wish I could have had some place to go to when I was a kid," Jennifer lamented.

"You were the fortunate one Naomi," she said.

She repeated, looking down into her plate as if she was looking back into her past to see if she had missed something, but knew nothing was there.

"My summers became what I lived for," Naomi recanted,

"They gave me the rare chance not to be cooped up at home where I was always alone. Despite the fact that we lived in a middle class neighborhood with all the trimmings, my summers use to save my social life."

"I could pretend that I was going away someplace different and tell the kids I went to school with whatever I wanted to tell them. Even though I only went to my Nana's house every summer and hung out with my friends in the country, it still was the place where I dreamed of living forever."

"Humph! Naomi said, most folk would rate Nana's house next to nothing more than a shack!" Jennifer the last bite of her fries while looking intently at Naomi who had almost stopped eating altogether.

"I'll bet you had fun," Jennifer said.

"I did, said Naomi. This house was on the highest scale in my young mind and I knew that someday it would be a safe haven of happiness for me."

"What do you mean about a safe haven for you," Jennifer asked?

"Were you in some kind of trouble?" Naomi clutched at her cloth napkin very tightly. Jennifer began looking a bit nervous and replied.

"You don't have to talk about this if you don't want to," she said.

"No," I am ok, I just hated the color blue for some strange reason and to top it off, my bed covers were blue as well with tiny stars with red stripes." Naomi realized she was repeating her entire life story to this stranger and couldn't understand why she thought of the color blue as if her mind was shifting from events earlier in her life. Jennifer realized Naomi had completely changed what she was talking about mid-sentence.

"Well, compared to mine, it still sounds like a great childhood to me."

"It was a way to survive," Naomi said, feeling once again as if her palms were becoming sweaty for no apparent reason. She briefly looked at her watch and chuckled.

"Well, I guess I have talked your head off, but thanks for listening."
"I think I will need a Togo box," can you get that for me. Naomi asked,
Jennifer looked at Naomi wondering if she was okay.
"Sure," I will get that for you. Before she turned to go and get the box, she asked Naomi a question...
"Maybe we can exchange numbers! I don't live too far from here and there aren't many young people in this town as you probably have noticed!" Naomi hurriedly scrambled in her pocket to find a piece of paper. When she couldn't; she began to perspire as if she was becoming faint once again.

It reminded her of the recurring dream she had where she couldn't find the light switch. Jennifer picked up on Naomi's emotions and changed the subject.
"Here...write it on this blank ticket, we won't tell my boss. I would love to get to know more about you and share some things about my boring life as well!" Naomi, finally calmed down, and smiled a nervous smile,
"I would like that Jennifer!"

"I will get that box for you...take care now! Naomi said her goodbyes and waited for the box. Jennifer had the waiter drop the box to Naomi because the rush dinner crowd was beginning to come in and she looked across the restaurant at Naomi and made a face that said she was getting swamped! Naomi nodded a nice smile and mouthed the words, "I understand" and did the call me hand gesture! She then packed her box and closed her purse after leaving Jennifer a huge tip on the ticket.

As Naomi walked out of the restaurant, there was a man coming through the door. He looked intently at Naomi as she walked out. She thanked him for holding the door open for her. He returned a shocked stare indicating that most people say nothing at all. Naomi had a lot to learn and it was only her first few months in the new town.

She had met her first friend and hoped this would be a good beginning...She thought about her Nana for a moment and decided she needed to concentrate on driving back to her apartment. It would be a good first day out on the town. Naomi hurried into her car and roll down the windows. It had become stuffy inside the car since she got out of it. She turned on her GPS and listened to the voice tell her how to get back to her apartment...she followed the directions and made it back to the complex and put in her code.

Cease To Exist

She was glad the place was gated. Even though it was all new to her living in a big city, she knew she wouldn't want to live where just anybody could walk up to her door. Turning the corner into her cul-de-sac, she found a parking spot and parked her car. She took the time to ensure she did not hit anyone's door. Lord, knows she hated for folks to hit her car doors. She then opened her back door of her sedan to get the doggy bag out she brought from the restaurant.

As she picked up the bag, it slipped from her hands and fell to the ground in the parking lot. "Doggone it!!! She said, in a hushed tone, hoping no one heard her. She was disappointed about what had just happened because she realized she hadn't eaten much and really cherished the idea of snacking on the tasty morsels from her meal at the restaurant.

So much for her midnight snack. Besides, she had no food in the apartment to speak of and didn't want to go back out after dark. Knowing she wanted to lose a few pounds she reasoned that eating at midnight was not the way to do it! Finally, she bent down to clean up the mess when two hungry pups out of nowhere came up to gobble up the dirty proceeds. They scurried up to her feet chomping on the morsels like it was their last meal. She almost envied them as they gobbled down the pieces of tender meat with the broccoli and dessert that she didn't order.

Author: Victoria E. Kain

She picked up the carton that the food came in and hurriedly walked up the walkway to the apartment door and pulled out her keys. Opening the door was easy and instantly the alarm began beeping. Naomi wasn't accustomed to alarms on doors. At home at Nanna's you just unlocked the door and walked in. Now she was panicking trying to remember the code…

"6385…"

"No"… 6835,

"Oh my goodness, she thought, my alarm is about to go off." As the beeps kept getting louder and louder in her head, she knew if she didn't hurry and get it right, the police would soon be at her door. Finally in a crucial moment, Naomi's heart was beating louder than the beeping on the alarm system…"

"Calm down and think, she thought to herself."

She tried one last time.

"6-5-3-8" ENTER… the beeping stopped and she dropped her purse on the floor and let out a loud sigh of relief closing the door quickly behind her.

She turned on the lights inside and hung the keys on the hook at the refrigerator as she walked into the living room kicking off her shoes as she entered. Naomi walked through the apartment and checked her closets and the back sliding door. She couldn't be too careful, living alone and all. This was the ritual she always performed when she came home. She never understood why she did it, she just did.

She had begun to felt sticky from standing in the parking lot and then at the door. It had been a muggy day being out and about in town and she desperately wanted to take a shower before she turned in. Turning on the T.V. just for noise, she picked up her cell phone, grabbed a pair of lounge pants and top out of the huge chest of drawers in her oversized closet and flipped her covers back on the bed.

The apartment complex was very cozy and the rooms were spacious. She turned on the light by the bed side and an instant smile came to her face as if she had accomplished something special, but she didn't understand why the smile. She checked the house phone for any messages but there weren't any. She thought her dad might have called while she was out.

Naomi went into the bath room and wrapped her hair up in a large towel. She began taking off her makeup and jewelry and put it on the granite counter. She turned on the shower to get the right temperature and selected the dial for pulsate to relieve some of the tension she had collected earlier from the day. Naomi undressed and slowly opened the door to the shower and stepped into the mini sauna. She closed her eyes and sat down on the seat and let the warm water run down her face. *Aaaaah,* she said…savoring the relaxation as she soaped her towel. The water felt great on her skin…

Naomi relaxed for a few minutes as time quickly passed by and she turned the water off and stepped out of the shower…Just as she is drying off, her phone rang…

"Who could that be?" she thought.

"Probably a wrong number."…now looking at the caller ID before answering and had no clue. When all else fails, she thought…

"Answer the phone!"

"Hello,"

"Hello… is this Naomi?"

"Yes it is, who is this?" Naomi quickly asked wondering who had her number.

"It's Jennifer, from the restaurant!"

"Wow!" Naomi thought.

"Did I leave something at the restaurant?" She asked, looking to see if her purse was in sight.

"Nooo, I am getting off shortly and my brother has my keys to the house so I can't get in for the next few hours."

"You mind me hanging out with you for the evening until he gets home?" "It won't be for long. I know it is really sudden, but since we had dinner together and all, I thought you might not mind. Technically I'm not a stranger." Jennifer recanted.

Naomi chuckled and relaxed a bit, thinking this was city life and she should get used to it. She initially wondered what this was about. She knew she didn't really know this woman, but had been so bold as to ask her to eat a meal with her.

She hadn't thought of having company tonight, especially someone she had just met, but decided if she was to get to know people, she needed to trust them and give them a chance to show themselves.

"Okay, as long as you are no closet serial killer," Naomi said, trying to make a joke and remembering Grandpa Cody's stale jokes that now mimicked hers. Jennifer laughed out loud.

"No, I stopped that a long time ago, I am straight now." They both laughed and Naomi gave her the address.

"I will be there in 15 minutes, my boss is giving me a ride."

"Ok," Naomi said, talking out loud as she hung up.

"Her boss?" What's up with that relationship, she thought. Maybe she will tell me tonight...maybe there is something going on between Jennifer and the boss, "hum?"

"Maybe, there is no brother to pick her up and this is just a line," still talking out loud to herself.

"Maybe I should just stop assuming that everyone is as weird as I am?"

Naomi went back and finished drying off hurriedly and got dressed...she put a bottle of wine in the fridge but didn't remember whether she liked wine or not... she just knew that she had some. She took out the chips and dip just in case her guest was hungry. She was not a good cook and had already eaten at the restaurant and that would have to serve her for the rest of the day. She decided to leave the snacks in the pantry and not sit them out but wanted to be prepared.

Naomi was almost giddy knowing she was having company for the first time at her new place since she arrived and it felt good. She thought about her Mama having company and understood why she was giddy. She never got to do this as a kid growing up with her mama…I hope this will be fun…I really do. She said, very anxious. Finally the doorbell rang. Not just once, but three times in succession as if someone was in a hurry.

Naomi looked out of the peep hole because this was her first visitor and the first time her door bell had rung as well. It is funny how people are about hearing a doorbell. They feel elated for some strange reason, and Naomi felt that same elation. She asked the proverbial question. "Who is it?" as if she didn't know…

"Hey lady, its Jennifer…open up!" Naomi opened the door and Jennifer rushed in laughing like a teenager. The car sped off through the complex.

"What was that about?" asked Naomi.

"This man is getting on my nerves," Jennifer lamented,

"I want to strangle him sometimes!" she said.

"I have told him time and again I am not interested in him and he just won't listen," she laughed and flicked her long straight hair from her face and flopped down on the sofa like a kid.

"Wow, nice place you got here!"

"Thanks, it will work for now."

"For now?" Jennifer was raising a brow.

"You must be loaded?"

"I sure couldn't afford something like this on my salary."

"I can only dream of living in this part of town too." She mumbled, as she walked around the apartment looking at everything as if she was in a museum.

"Well, it is a bit pricy," Naomi, reluctantly stated not knowing how she could afford it.

"So, what's the story about your boss Jennifer?" Naomi blurted out.

"Like I said," Jennifer repeated, as if being sarcastic and unnerved that she was being asked the question.

"He won't leave me alone!"

"You know what I mean…" looking down the front of her clothing.

"Well, you must have a lot of suitors as pretty as you are."

"Yeah, I guess you can say that, but I am really not ready to settle down yet, so I am as free as a bird." Jennifer said. Before Naomi could respond, Jennifer asked,

"Hey you got anything to eat around this swank joint?"

Naomi was glad that she had chilled the wine. She hurried to the pantry and took out the chips and got the dip and poured them separate bowls. When Naomi sat down, she asked Jennifer about her life.

There wasn't much to tell from Jennifer's standpoint, or maybe it was, but she didn't want to talk much about it. She was a bit evasive and Naomi noticed that when she asked about her mom and dad, she talked about her mom but when she spoke about her dad, she kept looking out towards the patio door like someone called her.

That was weird....Jennifer changed the subject and drank more wine and ate chips, and evaded the questions. She kept prodding Naomi to finish telling her story about her parents. It appeared she wanted to shift the attention from herself and insisted that she was more interested in Naomi's life... Naomi once again was talking about her own life to keep a conversation going.

"Well, not much to tell, except that... I was an inquisitive child and heard many things said by adults. The shocking part about hearing something when you are a child is that if you can remember what you heard, you can surely figure it out when you grow up."

"Trust me...you will figure it out." Naomi said.

"A lot of the things that I heard were about my mother's life. It was not until I was much older when I recalled these things I had heard and learned how my mother struggled through life as a wife and mother at the age of 15."

"15?" Jennifer yelled." She seemed disgusted at the thought.

"Oh "My Goodness," she said.

"Yes, 15," Naomi said, looking down at the carpet as if she had lost something of value there and couldn't find it.

She continued to talk about her life with this stranger slash soon to be friend. Naomi couldn't remember when the last time she had such an in-depth discussion about her family life and someone actually wanting to listen.

Naomi had almost come to tears, when she looked over at her guest, who had fallen fast asleep on the couch while she talked… At first she was shocked, but then realized that she was glad she didn't hear all the gory details of her life. Jennifer hadn't heard a thing she said. Maybe that was a good thing… She abruptly woke up and apologized.

"Lady, I am so tired!" I am at that stinky restaurant at 6 am in the morning! Benny always wants me there when he gets there…I am so sick of this…I am too young to be working like this…I should be living like you! I will someday, I will!" Naomi didn't know what to think about that statement.

She now looked around the apartment and realized that she must have been wealthy but didn't really know where her money came from…Jennifer asked for another glass of wine and Naomi got the bottle and poured the wine and Jennifer guzzled it down…It was a very expensive bottle which may have explained her drinking it so fast. Jennifer asked Naomi to tell her about her grandma as if she wanted a bed time story.

"Mine died when I was little," Jennifer said.

"So, hearing you talk about yours at the restaurant made me think of mine." "What I can remember…it gives me a good feeling." Naomi abruptly stopped her story and got up from sitting on the floor told Jennifer she needed to stretch her legs because they were getting a cramp in them.

Jennifer had gotten a bit tipsy from the wine. She looked over at Naomi and responded, "I know that's right!"

"But I am comfortable on this sofa." Naomi decided to move over to the oversized chair and took another sip of her wine. She was really feeling warm and sluggish. She tried to go on with the story about her life but there was a knock at the door…the two women looked at each other and frowned as if someone had the nerve to be knocking.

"Who can that be?"

"I hope it's not who I think it is." Jennifer said under her breath. Naomi went to the peep hole again and low and behold, it was Jennifer's boss. This time he was dressed up, as if he went home and changed to go on a date or something. Jennifer was feeling the wine effect fully and announced,

"Let me get the door if you don't mind, since its Benny."

Naomi was feeling a little light headed herself and rushed to get the spot on the sofa.

"No taking your spot back, you snoozed you lose!" she said.

Jennifer then opened the door and yelled at Benny.

"What do you want?"

"Can I talk to you for a minute?" Benny asked Jennifer.

"Not until you agree to give me a raise!" Jennifer demanded with a nervous laugh accompanied by a serious look and Benny agreed to her demands.

"Okay," a raise it is.

"Sooo…can we talk privately now?" Benny asked still peeking inside the living room trying to identify the woman sitting on the couch.

"Hey, isn't that the customer from the restaurant today," he asked Jennifer.

"That's right, so what?"

"We had an agreement," no fraternizing with the customers!"

"You idiot, this is my cousin!" She scolded him and lied.

"Well, you should have told me so" he sheepishly responded getting back to his original question.

"Can we talk now Jennifer?" he asked, again.

"Fine!" she said, showing disgust by his mere presence. She waived the okay sign at Naomi and told her she would be sitting out front in Benny's vehicle and would be right back.

Naomi got up and locked the door behind her just in case she didn't come back…she staggered over to the couch and flopped down again… Her head was now buzzing really heavy as she closed her eyes for a moment in anticipation of Jennifer coming back soon…A minute, five, thirty minutes went by. Naomi began to doze off. Finally she heard a knock at the door. Hurrying to get to the door thinking she would finish her conversation with Jennifer, she didn't check the peep hole anticipating who she thought it was and opened the door…

Author: Victoria E. Kain

As she swung the door open, a strange but very tall handsome man was standing in front of her. It was too late to close the door out of fear. Her heart was racing as she realized this was not Jennifer in her doorway. "Can I help you?" she asked. Naomi was holding her breath and watching his hands all at the same time to see if he would be going for anything in his pocket.

She had already spied out the vase on the table by the door rationalizing that if he made a sudden move, she could grab it and hit him once if it would help. Finally the man spoke.

"Hi, I am Jennifer's brother, Brock, I came to pick her up!" Naomi, began breathing again and leaned towards him and whispered.

"You scared me to death!!! I didn't know who you were and Jennifer is out talking with her boss in his car…I thought it was her knocking otherwise I would have looked out to see who it was first.

"May I come in and wait for her?" Brock asked, calmly checking Naomi out without being obvious.

"Well, I guess so, since you asked so politely," she said, being unusually coy. Brock walked in and Naomi offered him a glass of wine. Jennifer had left her cell phone on the sofa and Naomi picked it up and put it in her pocket for safe keeping. Brock sat down and began sipping the wine when Jennifer's cell phone rang. Naomi was reluctant to answer it and let it keep ringing. Finally out of annoyance, Brock asked if she was going to answer the phone.

Naomi smiled and politely excused herself and stepped into the kitchen. She pulled out the phone and looked at the caller ID. To her surprise, it said; "Big Brother, Paul" and had his picture on it. Naomi, was terrified now. 'Who was this man sitting in her living room that said he was Jennifer's brother if Jennifer's caller ID showed a different picture of a brother named Paul?'

"Oh, my lord, what am I going to do?" Naomi whispered under her breath.

"How will I get out of this...?" she thought.

"Is this man going to kill me...rape me, or both!!!?" Oh, my lord, where is Jennifer and why did she leave with her boss? Was this a set up???...she thought quickly getting more nervous as time passed.

Her first months in a big city and she would be on the front page of the New York Times. She kept thinking..."was that really Jennifer's boss?" Suddenly, Naomi realized she had the phone in her hand so why not call 911. After all, the man was in the living room and not in the kitchen with her. Just when she was about to dial 911, Brock entered the kitchen door way.

"Hey, can I get some ice?" Naomi dropped the phone on the floor and Brock slowly reached down to pick it up. Naomi was speechless as the phone rang again... "Oh, no!" she thought, he will know that I know he is not Jennifer's brother now that he has the phone. The picture of the other man came up again, and Brock looked at it and answered the phone.

"What do you want little brother?"

"Yeah, I am here to pick up Jennifer," he calmly stated.

"She's out talking to that jerk of a husband," he said to Paul on the phone. Finally Naomi could breathe again. She had almost fainted from relief. She sat down at the kitchen counter and poured another glass of wine and took a big sip…she really had been scared out of her wits thinking it was all over. Brock hung up the phone.

"I bet Jennifer didn't tell you she had two brothers?"

"No, she didn't, Naomi said."

"That girl is a mess"…Brock stated, shaking his head in disbelief. Brock and Naomi went back into the living room and sat down. She was relaxed now and felt much better but wanted Jennifer to come in from outside. The whole thing was very awkward for her now. She turned to Brock,

"Can you check on Jennifer, she has been out there a long time with her boss?"

"Jennifer will be out there for a while." It was apparent Naomi had not heard him say that Benny was Jennifer's husband.

"You see, if she has not told you, Benny is actually Jennifer's husband not her boss. They didn't tell anyone because Jennifer was only 16 when she got pregnant and he had to marry her. Benny realized that his restaurant franchise would suffer if he told anyone that he was married to a 16 year old. So they kept their marriage a secret and she works as his manager/waitress so they could be seen together as her employer.

Cease To Exist

People thought he was just promoting one of his employees. Jennifer ended up having a miscarriage but Benny didn't want to annul the marriage. He really loved her I guess. "He is dealing with it because Jennifer is still very young. I am glad my mother was not here to witness all this. It would have broken her heart. My dad insisted that this man not take advantage of Jennifer and Benny agreed to put her through college and buy her whatever she wanted. Dad was still alive then and would have killed him if he didn't. After they were married, dad died. And here we are!

"We are wealthy by way of Benny's money." Naomi was stunned to learn that Jennifer was married to this old man…and only four years ago. No wonder she was able to sit so long at the diner without getting fired…Naomi thought. That explains it. That makes me four years older than her, Naomi thought. "Wow!" Brock went on to talk about how they grew up very poor and had to admit that Jennifer marrying this man made things financially better for them initially.

"Jennifer's husband paid the house off which gave us a place to live."

"My brother Paul and I were in college and Benny paid for that as well. I think she stayed with him to help us all out. If he dies, we will be very wealthy, Brock said.

"What about you Naomi?"

"You haven't said much about yourself, Brock said."

"Here I go again telling my story."

Author: Victoria E. Kain

"I had begun telling your sister about my life and she went to sleep on me while I was talking."

"Well, I promise I won't go to sleep if you talk about you." Smiling a big smile, Brock made long eye contact with Naomi. Naomi went on to fill him in on her life and had enough time to finish before Jennifer returned. Brock listened intently and seemed to enjoy having the opportunity to look at Naomi while she spoke. He complimented her on how well spoken she was and used an old cliché.

"Was your mother an English teacher?"

She quietly blushed and told him no, but that she really appreciated the compliment. This was the first time a man had paid that kind of special attention to Naomi and she was enjoying it.

"That was an amazing story you just told me," Brock changed the subject quickly."

"Please don't tell me you are the same age as my sister?"

"Well…no, I am 24," Naomi said.

"I am 29." Brock jumped in, as if he was in line for something free. Just when their conversation was beginning to be about them, the doorbell rang again. Brock, sat mesmerized and watched Naomi get up to answer the door. He commented again about her life.

"I wish I had good memories like yours," he said.

"You are fortunate Naomi."

Naomi smiled a strange smile not knowing why this did not feel much like a compliment coming from Brock…she reached the front door and this time, looked through the peep hole first to make sure it was Jennifer. Opening the door, Jennifer stormed in like a child abruptly saying her goodbyes to Naomi and smirking at her brother as if he had done something wrong by being there.

"I guess you got to hear the end of my story from big mouth here, Jennifer asked Naomi?" rolling her eyes at Brock.

"Yes I did," Naomi replied.

"Since you were detained, as usual…are you ready to go?" Brock asked.

"Yep, gotta get to the restaurant early in the morning. I am a new V.P. for the Restaurant.

"I'll meet you in the car!"

Jennifer didn't even look at Naomi. Brock made a face and stopped in front of Naomi as Jennifer all but slammed her front door.

"Can I come by to visit you sometimes?" he asked.

"Maybe I can get to know you better."

"Well, maybe," Naomi said. Not knowing how far she wanted to take this strange relationship.

"Well, you have my number," if you'd like company sometimes, give me a call."

"I am not married either... Just thought I would let you know that." Brock winked at Naomi and said goodnight.

Naomi closed the door and finally dressed for bed. She realized she had had a heck of a day. 'I've told my life history to total strangers today, she thought,' but it somehow made her feel better. There was still something strange about how she told the story to Jennifer about Nana... it was as if she was actually there with her... She checked the locks and set her alarm clock.

Jumping in bed, she scrunched up her pillows knowing that the three glasses of wine would soon have her sound asleep...Everything was quiet in her new place that night...Soon, in the wee hours of the morning, she heard a horrible loud noise from inside her room...Her dream this night seemed to fast forward and the deafening noise made time stand still.

The sound of a clock kept ticking louder and louder in Naomi's head until it completely woke her up from a dead sleep. Perspiration was pouring from her face as she sat straight up in her bed in the dark. Trying to determine where she was and why it was so hot and stuffy in her room, she thought she had left the window open for ventilation before she went to sleep, but quickly realized that she was not at Nana's.

She had been startled out of her sleep but couldn't remember why. Naomi noticed that the room smelled like a musty wool blanket. It was still dark in the room as she searched for the light switch that should have been right beside her bed.

Cease To Exist

She felt that if she could see what was going on in the room she wouldn't be frightened anymore, but began to feel a cold chill come over her. She knew that time was running out and she had to wake up fully or it would be too late. Naomi mumbled in a low voice, "Where is that stupid light switch?" She was beginning to feel as if the room was closing in on her. Before she could finish one thought, another one flooded her mind.

"What's that smell?" She frantically searched alongside her bed trying to examine her covers to determine the awful smell. Now she began flailing in a desperate sweeping motion until finally, the sound of thunder came crashing in the distance and broke her futile quest to find the light switch. She gave up with a sigh of relief after hearing the heavy drops of rain falling outside on the rooftop. The soothing raindrops caused her to reason that she had a bad dream and no longer needed to turn the light on.

Naomi lay lifeless on the bed, exhausted from the struggle that had taken place. She continued to hear the sound of the falling rain trying to remember what the dream had been about before she was abruptly awakened. Soon she gave up all thoughts for sleep. The last thing she remembered was hearing the thunder echoing in the distance. Her thoughts soon faded into the darkness as she fell asleep… Naomi would never remember the previous day's events again.

Author: Victoria E. Kain

She would succumb to the darkness and give in to the night. What was this thing that had haunted her from childhood until now? Why was her life events being repeated over and over again? Soon, very soon she would have the answers once and for all and it could be laid to rest. Naomi!?... Naomi! The voice kept calling in a soft whisper in the distance. Once again, she was forced to awaken herself from this deep sleep that would entomb her. There was a heavy weight on her chest and she could barely move.

Slowly, she opened her eyes... squinting to filter out the bright sun light that was beaming down on her face from an enormous bay window in a strange room she occupied. Having no recollection of how she got there, she raised herself erect and looked around the beautiful room. She was puzzled, but stretched out her arms any way and gradually greeted the morning sun. The room was very pretty and she could feel a slight breeze coming in through the open window.

She now remembered leaving it open but couldn't remember why. She could see the curtains moving back and forth as she lay silent on the bed trying to determine where she was and what was happening to her mind. "Why do I feel as if I am still asleep?" she wondered. She knew she was not fully awake but could do nothing about it. Examining the room she is in, she saw things that were vaguely familiar and other things looked strange. 'Whose voice had whispered her name?'

Who had awakened her this time to keep her in the land of the living?" Instinctively, she turned over and lay flat on the bed looking in the direction of her night table. Her eyes searched the hand carved lamps that graced the table and it felt familiar.

Where did this table come from? Have I been to an Island? Her eyes kept searching the lamp until it frightened her as she pondered why such an interest in the table so suddenly. Every minute she tried to think about something, her head would begin pounding instantly.

Finally, the telephone rang and startled her. Still in a daze, she let the answering machine pick up the call. "Naomi! Naomi!" the voice said. Trying to see if it was the same voice that had awakened her, Naomi did not pick up. Maybe, the phone rang while I was asleep and woke me up, she thought, as she listened to the caller's voice.

"It's Brock, pick up if you are there!" Naomi did not pick up. She did not know who this person was but was intrigued by his voice. The caller went on to state that they would pick her up at 8pm because there was bad weather in Texas. They had an early flight schedule and she should be dressed on time. The last statement was of concern to Naomi.

"I Love you," the caller said. Naomi began smiling as she looked down at the phone as if the voice she heard had meant something to her, yet she could not recall who this was.

She got up from the bed and went towards the closet vaguely remembering a beautiful dress. She opened the door and a recording sounded. "Please close door to jewelry box three." She looked over to close the drawer, puzzled as to how she knew where it was. She looked in the drawers and saw beautiful diamond rings, bracelets and pearls. Out of sheer curiosity, she tried on a bracelet and was stunned by its beauty.

Quickly she removed it and looked around the room to see if anyone had seen her. She felt she was in the wrong place. This man Brock had said that he had bought a dress for her a week earlier that the tag was still on it. Naomi now looked for the dress that had a tag. She finally saw a gorgeous dress and tried it on. She looked at the tag and gasped at the price. 'Where in the world did he get this dress from and why did he pay so much money for it? She reasoned Brock must be important and very wealthy.

Naomi was intrigued by the thought of being the center of attention for once in her life. Was it conceit or just plain foolishness? She couldn't wait for the day to be over with and the night to fall so that she would see this man Brock at the event. She dressed for shopping and felt that she was sitting on top of the world. Finally leaving her room, she walked out of the door of her huge estate and a man approaches her and brought her car around.

Naomi's day was happy and busy with shopping for accessories and only the finest perfumes. It was as if her life was on remote control. She was doing things she did not understand, but moving mechanically through her life in a shadows. Everything seemed to go in slow motion. She had lunch with a close friend who owned a restaurant chain, whose husband had passed away and left her very wealthy. They had a glass of wine together and Naomi soon left.

The way things looked to Naomi, this life was the best ever and nothing could spoil what she was thought she had at this moment. She finished shopping and came home with boxes and bags her driver brought in for her. The downstairs maid drew a bath for her. It's late in the afternoon and she wanted to be well rested for the nights' event. Naomi finished her bath and draped a plush robe around her.

She laid across the bed to relax looking up at the ceiling. Closing her eyes, she remembered the dress she had seen earlier in her closet. She couldn't wait for the fireworks to begin that evening and slowly drifted into a deep sleep. This time, her sleep would end forever. Her efforts to relax would quickly fade tragically. She became restless and the dreams came back. She was taken to a lonely time in her life. Remembering that her mother never came back to see her grow up as a child. This was a pivotal moment for her.

Author: *Victoria E. Kain*

She had endured much in her young years, living with her interracial parents who pretended to be happy in the eyes of onlookers, but behind the scenes, her mother did not love her or her father. Naomi had witnessed firsthand her father's love while he was alive, but remembered that her mother's lover had killed her father when he returned home from overseas unannounced. This was a sad time in her life... In her dream, she wished her mother had not left her and her dad when she was young.

She saw herself walking towards her mother and her mother called out her name in a hushed voice...Her mother then gently whispered something to her that sounded like, "It's time to go now." But this time, Naomi couldn't make out what was being said... She tried to understand the words her mother was speaking to her but became irritated knowing that her mother was the cause of her father's death.

She was angry with her mother and had never told her how she felt. Finally, in the dream, Naomi's mother walked up to her abruptly and shoved Naomi away from her onto the floor in the darkened room. In a desperation, Naomi cried out. She missed her father and her Nana and her mother, even though her mother was still alive, she never came back to see her. It was as if Naomi had ceased to exist in her mother's eyes.

She began to cry harder as her heart began to race. Suddenly, she heard a door slam shut behind her and she was alone in the darkness once again. She remembered how her mother use to make her stay in her room when she had company and how she hated it. A flood of memories returned to Naomi and the dream was becoming out of control. She was remembering everything now as clear as a bell. Fragmented pieces came to her…her dolls at her Nanna's house that she loved so much and how she treasured going to her grandparents' home every summer.

Her memory was coming back to her as flashes of light kept surging through her brain like an underground tunnel. Her life was being hurled back to her from the time she was in Germany and to the day that she left for college but never arrived. Finally, she couldn't shake the memories anymore but her body was trying to raise up from the bed as her brain continued to click through time bringing her closer and closer to reality and the moment she was now in.

It seemed that she was beginning to remember current events of being at the restaurant and could remember the people walking down the street….she tried harder to stay in the moment as her mind began to wane in and out. She knew that if she stopped remembering, she would never wake up again. In desperation, she flails in her sleep in the dark, reaching for anything to hold on to as she felt the weightlessness of her body like as if she was falling from a cliff.

Now frantic, knowing that the life force was slowly leaving her, if she does not awaken soon, she will be lost forever. Exhaustion has taken over her brain and its ability to feed more memory to bring her back to the living…In her heart, she quietly resolves that she will give up the fight once and for all and give in to the quietness of the dark place that contains her. She was tired of the dreams she had been forced to endure that she couldn't understand.

'Sleeping forever may not be so bad if you never wake up,' she thought.

She stopped fighting to give in to being lost forever. She began to let go……..Suddenly… she hears a faint sound like a clock ticking that was getting louder and louder. The sound resonates in her senses. "TICK, TOCK… TICK…TOCK," the sound was as if someone was walking along a fence with a stick making the sound as it passed over each opening one by one, faster and faster. Finally, the ticking noise became so loud Naomi could no longer take the pressure of the sound.

Her body began surging violently out of control until she is shoved by some invisible force into an upright position in her bed. Gasping for air, she groped for the light switch once again to halt the darkness not realizing she only had to open her eyes. Still flailing she falls to the floor. Now with her eyes wide open, she remembers the musty odor of the wool blanket and can see it on the bed. The smell is more pronounced now with the reality that she is in the darkened room.

Fear griped her like an iron fist as she desperately searched in a sweeping motion trying to find her way back up on the bed but ended up on the opposite corner of the room. The floor is cold and hard. Her efforts are futile, but now, Naomi is fully awake for the first time and very afraid of her surroundings. Her eyes moved mechanically back and forth in the dark like a deranged person knowing she was fully awake and not dreaming. This time, out of shear desperation to find out what is happening to her, she calms' herself as she sits shivering in the corner of the tiny room.

She soon hears a siren go off in the distance with a deafening tone. It is followed by a blinding bright light now illuminating the tiny space exposing her positon as she hovers in the corner on the dingy concrete floor. Her eyes follow the light, as she slowly opens and closes them, squinting and shielding her face from the new element her brain is now adjusting to. A voice out of nowhere is heard that she does not recognize.

What she hears next causes her to hover between the real and unreal. Over an intercom, the voice repeats…*"ALL PRISONERS STEP OUT OF YOUR CELLS FOR INSPECTION!"* The voice is commanding and Naomi scrambles to obey it. She tries to get up on her feet but loses her balance due to physical weakness of having been bed ridden for years.

She immediately falls down on the bed to avoid falling on the cold floor again. In a blood curdling scream, she repeats what the guard has announced. "Prisoner!!!" She exclaims..., now shivering violently! The cruel reality slammed Naomi square in the face. She stood up again with the light now shining directly down on her room. She can finally see the musty wool blanket laying partially on her tiny bed and the concrete floor.

The smell was a stench to her, even in her dreams. She realized that this was the smell that she could never identify and when she searched for the light switch, she could not find one because it did not exist in the prison that housed her. It all had been a dream. This dream, unlike others, had kept Naomi alive for many years. The prison guards made their rounds and walked over to Naomi's cell and was surprised to see her awake. They asked her to finally face the bars. They made a quick call to the doctor that had been treating her these years.

The quiet place that had entombed here would soon be a shadow of her memory and the nightmarish dreams would cease to exist forever. She beaconed for one of the guards and in a shaky voice asking them where they were taking her.

"How long have I been here?" she pleaded for an answer.

The guard laughed a smug laugh and responded.

"I have been working at this women's prison for 14 years and you have been here for 6 of those years." Naomi was devastated by the guards' response and fell to the floor.

They guards rushed in and collected Naomi taking her to the infirmary. This time, unlike all others, she no longer returned to the catatonic state she had been in. She instantly was revived and regained consciousness. They radioed for the doctor who had attended Naomi to inform her that her patient was finally awake. They all thought that Naomi would die in the state she was in and only did the basics for her. No one could figure out why this doctor had almost devoted her life to what they thought was a total stranger to her.

They had never understood the connection until now. Naomi was an inmate, but was put first on the doctors list of patients every day that she came into the prison to provide medical care for them all. Once in the infirmary, they got Naomi to sit up on the side of the bed. The noise was very loud now with all the inmates trying to wake up after being roused from their sleep.

Many of them were no older than Naomi when she first came in. She kept repeating, "6 years," over and over again, but now with tears rolling down her cheeks. A sick feeling came up in the pit of her stomach causing her to feel nauseated. What am I in here for? She pondered…quietly trembling. She was puzzled as to why she had been imprisoned for these years. Tears still rolling down her cheeks as she looked up at the warden and now the physician who was standing next to her.

Author: Victoria E. Kain

She quietly asked, looking at the warden as if to get permission to ask the question... "Why, why me?" Naomi felt that her life was over. She glanced over at the physician who looked intently at her, but did not speak. She looked familiar to Naomi but she was unsure of everything at this point. The questions she had would have to be answered or she surely would sink back into the deathlike state she had been in. The physician and the warden walked over to the opposite side of the room and whispered intently. Naomi was beginning to feel faint again and did not know what to do at this point.

Darkness was beginning to take over again...but this time, she would welcome it. She would allow it to swallow her up forever....as she began to let go of the life that she had fought so hard to keep, she was fading into darkness once again...she hears the familiar voice that had softly awakened her from her sleep..."Naomi, Naomi... "Stay with me Naomi!" It demanded. Naomi, was groggy and weak.

"Do you remember me?" the physician asked. Naomi looked up at the physician and searched her kind face. The physician held Naomi's hand in both of hers and looked into her eyes. Finally Naomi's eyes opened wide and she burst into tears...she recognized the face of her childhood friend, Shellie.

"Shellie? Shellie...Is it really you?"

Cease To Exist

"It is me, Naomi," I have been here with you all along! Shellie and Naomi hugged each other and cried. The warden looked on in disbelief at what Shellie had done for her friend. This moved him to tears as he walked out of the room to give them time alone. Naomi's life was coming back to her in pieces. She began remembering the dreams and how they had continued to repeat themselves.

This is what kept her alive. The dreams would go from childhood to her adult life with Brock who she now realized was "her" abusive husband. Once Shellie had examined Naomi and determined she was gaining full memory back, she conveyed information to Naomi about her life. Shellie told Naomi that in her dreams, Naomi had thought that it was "Shellie's" mom who was abused, but in reality, it was Naomi. Naomi was married to Brock who had given Naomi all the luxuries of life. Brock had become wealthy by way of his sister's inheritance when Benny passed away, leaving Jennifer with the entire Restaurant Franchise. Naomi's life was unhappy. She wanted to know more and Shellie would tell it all.

Brock was wealthy but he also was an alcoholic. Her dream of Shellie's father who was an alcoholic mimicked her own real life with her husband Brock. Naomi's husband would beat her and then buy her pretty things to make up for the beatings.

Author: Victoria E. Kain

The abuse became more severe each time he got drunk. Naomi could not deal with her horrible life but took the abuse for many years because she had nowhere to go. Her Nana and Grandpa Cody were gone as well as her father. Shortly after their third wedding anniversary, Naomi found out she was pregnant. She was happy about the pregnancy but Brock didn't care and continued to beat her after each alcoholic binge.

Months went by during the pregnancy and one night, Brock came home and started a fight with Naomi. She was seven months pregnant at the time and he hit her so hard that she almost lost consciousness. When she tried to stand up, Brock hit her again with one blow to her stomach and she fell unconscious. She did not remember anything until she woke up the next morning in the hospital. She realized she had bruises all over and a fractured wrist. The doctors told Naomi that she had delivered a baby girl prematurely. She was happy thinking the baby would be okay, because she was alive.

But when she saw the baby's frail body in the incubator, Naomi began to cry. She rubbed her tiny hands and stroked her hair. Naomi watched her baby lay helpless in the hospital for days. She cried each time she saw her, remembering that the doctors said it had a lot to do with the injury Naomi sustained to her abdomen. Naomi realized that it was her dreams during the coma that produced an escape from her pain.

Cease To Exist

Shellie went on to recall Naomi's lost life to her. Naomi's husband was the one who had injured their beautiful baby. Choosing not to leave the hospital, Naomi stayed every day for two weeks. Holding her little girl as often as she could. During that time, her husband never came home to see the baby. On that October morning, Naomi went home to get a change of clothing and picked up a blue sweater for her little girl. The hospital called for her to come quickly. When Naomi arrived at the hospital. Little Mattie was barely alive.

She had decided to name her after her Nana…it was the least she could do. After an hour of gasping for breath, Naomi held Mattie's tiny hands one final time and was permitted to kiss her baby goodbye, as she slipped away. Naomi was devastated. The hospital staff could not contain her distress and had to sedate her and kept her overnight. It would be the darkest night and day of her life.

The next morning, she finally left the hospital and returned home hoping her husband would be there to learn of their baby girl's death. He did not come home at all. Days went by and Naomi made the arrangements to bury her baby. After the services, she had been given pills to sleep and had taken them for her pain. As she lay in her bed half awake, she heard the front door open. Elated, thinking her husband was finally home to console her, she would soon be greeted by a cold fist to her shoulder. He then drug her out of bed, slinging her to the floor. She tried to get up, but the pills had sapped her strength. Naomi cried out in a loud shrill….

Author: Victoria E. Kain

"OUR BABY IS DEAD...MATTIE, IS DEAD!!!" She screamed. In a drunken stupor, Brock laughed and taunted Naomi..."Well you are about to join her..." he said, cold and uncaring. It was then that Brock raised his fist and knocked Naomi to the floor again...Naomi picked up the fireplace iron and yelled, "NO MORE!!!" She swung it as hard as she could and hit Brock one time. He fell to the floor and did not move.

Naomi was screaming and the neighbors came to her door. They heard what had happened and called an ambulance and the police. The carpet was soaked with blood and she now remembered the tiny bed she slept in even though they lived in a mansion. She had been forced to sleep in the basement of the home which had concrete floors. A flood of memories and the reality of Naomi's brutal life came back to her as Shellie finished telling her what happened to her.

The warden walked back into the hallway and called out her name… "Naomi, Naomi," Kilpatrick, please come this way!" Reaching for her delicate hands, they removed the hand cuffs and shackles off her feet. Naomi looked up at Shellie for reassurance. She nods in agreement with the warden's action. Naomi was finally free to go home. A flood of tears roll down Naomi's cheeks as she buried her tired body on the shoulder of her friend. She whispered, "I remember, I remember it all!" She remembered the dreams that had kept her alive for those years in prison.

Cease To Exist

The dreams of all the good times as a little girl were part of the lost years of her life. Soon she would be able to put the pieces together and unwind her soul. She remembered little Mattie and shed tears. To her utter delight, Shellie had been with her the entire time. From the summer they came back from Germany and Shellie's brother was killed in Vietnam, Shellie went away for a while. The man that survived the war that was with Shellie's brother when he was killed, met Shellie and they were married that next summer she was home.

Shellie had decided to go to medical school and became a doctor. One day while reading the newspaper, Shellie noticed the story about Naomi's wealthy husband Brock being killed and Naomi being charged with his murder. Naomi couldn't take the loss of her baby and now the death of her husband by her hand even though it was self-defense. She was too weak to fight and was imprisoned and slipped into a coma. Since Naomi could not testify, they would leave her locked up until she either died or came to in order to plead her own innocence. Shellie immediately transferred her practice to Canoga Springs to work in the prison with Naomi.

She worked out a plan with the correctional facility to try a new medical discovery that would keep the brain alive in coma patients by introducing positive life experiences on a repetitive basis. She worked hard every day and the procedure had worked on Naomi. Shellie had been the one feeding Naomi the information from her childhood which supported the positives in her dreams.

Author: Victoria E. Kain

It was truly a miracle! Today, Naomi would walk out of the prison doors, realizing she had ceased to exist in her past life but was alive again to have a new future. They acquitted her of all charges of murder. Shellie's love and loyalty kept Naomi alive. The two of them would walk out of the prison doors together that day and the sunlight would never been brighter. Shellie's husband Paul drove the car around to the entrance of the prison that had held Naomi captive in her mind for six long years.

He welcomed Naomi back and helped her into the back seat of the car. Shellie entered the other passenger door and sat in the back with her friend. She wanted to give her the support she would need, letting her know her safety would never be an issue again. Naomi sat motionless in the backseat of the car the same as she did when she was a child. The sound of the car engine startled her and instincts caused her to grab hold of Shellie's hand for security. Like a compassionate friend, Shellie calmed Naomi and reassured her that she would always be by her side.

They slowly drove out of the prison gates. A soft breeze rushed over Naomi's face causing her eyes to close as she soaked in the beauty of her new found freedom. Her every move was guarded as she leaned back on the seat allowing her body to relax. Quickly recoiling to ensure that the dreams were gone forever. This time, she knew it was real.

Naomi was weary from the long ordeal and stared through the tinted glass watching the links of the barb wired fence quickly go by with each gear that the car changed. There was a homeless man slowly walking alongside a chain link fence holding a stick in one hand. He was systematically striking each opening one by one.

The image caused Naomi to sit up and take notice, remembering that the sound she heard in her dream was this same sound the man was making outside her prison wall. It was the sound that had awakened her from sleeping forever that day. As they passed him by, she looked through the rear glass window and saw the man raise his hand and wave goodbye. As she settled back into the seat, the car moved faster and faster down the highway. That day, Naomi vowed in her heart never to allow anyone to make her feel invisible again. Soon the image of the prison was no longer in sight. She was fully awake this time and completely back in the land of the living…This time…it was for good.

THE END…or, is it?

Author: Victoria E. Kain

"What is a spider without its web?"